MW01139915

The Smell of Breath

A love story… sort of

Conor McMillen

Forward by Brittany Taylor.

I am Conor's partner, lover, friend and, to use the parlance of our time, his baby-momma. I was honored when Conor asked me if I would write the forward for his novel, this novel, The Smell of Breath, and delighted, as I have enjoyed being a part of the process of it all coming together. Also, because of my position, I feel I can offer a unique perspective on what I find to be a truly beautiful piece of work.

Over the years, one of my favorite things to ask Conor about has been the relationships he has experienced throughout his life, and particularly his romantic partners that existed before we knew one another. I have found it to be one of my favorite ways to connect with Conor on a heart level. I've enjoyed the details of how he has shared about each love or lust, whether they were in his life for a night or stuck there since boyhood. I love the look in his eye as he shares, the tone of his voice, his body language, and have relished in paying attention to the ways various parts of him come alive in the reminiscing of it all. It has been one of the most beautiful ways I have enjoyed being transported into Conor's mind, his heart, his soul, his life-path and his unique expression. It has felt like such an intimate journey, leading through the core of his being, while still on a deeper level, reflecting the experiences I imagine so many other humans have had.

As Conor was putting this novel together, he would read me excerpts in the car as we drove somewhere, or in the evening as we lay in bed. I was always eager to hear his words, his story, read through his voice, and feel us both transported in time. I found myself craving more, craving to venture again into a previous time in his life, craving to experience the emotion of it all, craving to feel more of Conor through his words, a place where I have felt him come alive perhaps more than anywhere else.

I also loved trying to guess who each segment was about; which special person and experience Conor was calling forth to paint the pages with their essence and his, from his perspective, during a particular moment or memory. When I read the whole novel through on my own, pretending to be a reader who had never known these love stories as I did, the mystery of knowing who was who remained in a new way, and I liked that. I imagined being a new reader with the feeling of curiosity, wondering which character was which, if someone new was coming along, if I would get to know the end of this or that person's story, if we would come back to it further along in the novel, or where the journey was headed. As the novel continued, I found myself enjoying how it all unfolded, how the pieces did come together, and recognized I would really want to encourage readers to enjoy the storytelling, the potential mystery at times, and the development of it all.

The interweaving of stories, the uniqueness and simultaneous universal-truths of the themes Conor shares about hit deeply on the raw emotion of what it means for so many to be human, to be a lover, to be a searcher, to be filled with desire, to be filled with questions, to feel full, to feel empty, to be a human in love and out of love and in love over and over again, throughout a journey of self discovery.

I am so proud of this being, this novel, and the energy that Conor chooses to share with the world each day. It is a joy knowing him. And, though I may be slightly biased, I feel that he is amongst the greatest writers I have ever read, and I am continually blown away by how he can capture the subtleties and depth of the human experience through his words, as he has in this novel, The Smell of Breath.

-Brittany Taylor

This is not fiction. But I'm also not sure if it happened this way. I know memory is creative.

1.

There are some things I want to tell you. Some things you don't know about me. Some things that happened when you were changing and when I was changing and that thing we did together... That thing… Do you remember it? It had changed and it was done and distant and also close and dead and also new and I was inside of it and also outside of it. There are so many stories from this time and so many places and so many people and so many feelings it is hard to know where to start and harder to know what to keep in and what to leave out. It is impossible to know where it all begins or ends or even to see it through my own eyes. Sometimes I feel like I am far away from it and watching it all happen to someone else. Sometimes - I know you know this - sometimes stories are just poems. Sometimes they are conversations. Sometimes they are not even correct - the facts innocently malformed over time. And sometimes they are truthful in a way that extends beyond truth. Does that make sense? These stories, they get stuck; they repeat themselves. They can be messy. And this is, I believe, all because they are still playing themselves out inside of us when we think of them and when we share them. They are not really in the past, are they?

And so this is how I'll write these stories - in the way that they come and are endless and finite and mine and someone else's and strings of words shared and poems and memories. Perhaps by the end you will know me a little more. And perhaps, more importantly, I will, too.

2.

I was lying on the asphalt with a girl beside me whose arm was touching my arm through a few layers of jackets and our heads were looking upward at a sky full of stars. Some were moving and we saw a total of six that really moved and that first one was the best. She looked at me and then back at the sky and in that moment I smelled her breath. The smell of breath. The way breath smells. I felt it. Warm with some cigarette and so human and so female and sweet. I wanted to get inside that breath with my mouth and swallow it whole over and over and leave my tongue inside of her mouth and breathe in and feel the humid taste of her breath inside me.. I wanted to be with her and I had no idea how to be with anyone but you. It was confusing and exciting and all I could do was look at the stars and just keep inhaling.

And in this moment, I miss the smell of breath in the night when you are sleeping. When I am awake near you so close that breath touches my nose and my cheeks. When I am watching you. When you are making small noises like a child and you are holding your pillow or your knees or you are reaching for me like a child reaches in memory of her mother's breast or mouth or breath. When, in that way you reach for me, I am there and you stay sleeping. When you are simple. When you are nothing but a girl. Just a small girl in a bed with me in a night that is dark and nothing else exists outside of it. I miss the smell of breath.

When I decided to go back to school I did it because I felt I had to become something more than what I was. The only path I knew was a reflection of something I thought you wanted in me, a career that made more money and was far away from anything that could be considered working class. I hired a tutor on Craigslist to help me study math so I could pass the LSATs and apply for architecture school. Do you remember her? I think you met her a couple of times. She was awkward and nerdy and hip and sexy in a grunge sort of way. She was taller than me and smoked cigarettes and ate Swedish Fish and had a dog named Newton and a boyfriend that lived in another state she was feeling distant from. And she tutored me for a while and then we became friends and then she became the first girl I really wanted to kiss. I wanted everything with her, really, because I had no filter for relationships and no dating experience and no concept of making moves or sharing intimacy. I never kissed her. And I never took the LSATs. And eventually her boyfriend moved back to town and they ended up renting the house in Belchertown while I went here and there and even lived in the garage next to them for a while. He was a really nice guy. I wonder if she ever told him that she and I lay out one night and looked at the stars and that the tension between us was palpable. Maybe she just told him she thought I was a decent dude who was pretty sad and who she was doing a favor by spending extra time with. Or maybe she didn't think to tell him anything at all.

4.

(talks with men)

"How was it?"

"Good."

"Yeah?"

"Yeah, no it was. She's uhm. Well she's, she's cute. So that's good. I was really worried about it. I didn't show you her pictures but like three of them were super cute and then the last one was like 'uhm. Hmm. Maybe you shouldn't have posted that one.' And that one was the only one that was a close up of just her face like head on. So anyway... she was cute, that was good. But she reminds me a little bit of my sister. Which is weird."

"Huh. Yeah."

"Yeah. And like little things, you know- not a big deal- I don't know what the fuck I'm complaining about she was totally cute and nice and smart and pretty funny and has her shit together so I should just shut the fuck up... It was just little things, you know."

"What did you guys do?"

"Went to the cafe. She got a milkshake. I got a water. Then we took a walk. It was hot."

"Did you feel a connection with her?"

"Nah... No, but she was cute."

It was Saturday night in summer in the Pioneer Valley. It had been over a hundred degrees for three days in a row and then dropped to seventy and the clouds came out of the earth and over the mountains like giants throwing bolts of lightning, their boots thundering and then the rain came down in thick black sheets. He was waiting inside the market just a moment longer to see if it would break or slow or stop. He didn't know it wouldn't stop until the morning. So he waited and looked at the produce that lined the walls. Tomatoes and avocados and celeriac bulbs. *Sell-air-e-ack,* he said it to himself, looking at the large white bulbs, the long tails of stalk. *Sellaireack. Sellaireack. Sellaireack.* He thought of a day at the old house. They'd been outside in the sun gardening.

"This is the weirdest plant. It looks like celery but it tastes kind of gross. Taste this."

"Licorice - weird. Is it edible?"

"I don't know. Probably but it's not very good. Should I pull it?"

"Eh. Let's see what it does."

And then the day had gone on and then the sun went down and the house became *the old house* and the night took them and placed them into separate beds with blankets and loneliness. Empty beds with no legs entangled in legs and arms around chests and hands on breasts and heads on shoulders, just pillows cradled and cats pulled close and thick edges of sadness in the grooves and sweat that is fear and sleep that is restless and then the sun came up. And two people become alone and gone, lost among a herd of people lost and gone and alone and they are no longer anything that they were.

The old house. Celeriac. That's what that shit was. He looked up and through the window. The rain hadn't changed. Sheets of black and the air, that haunting blue-green. A few people ran with bags of groceries to their cars, keys ready. It still took time to unlock the door and they got soaked and running is useless. He sighed and walked to the door slowly, his bag of groceries bumping against the side of the bins of vegetables. He looked like a child with nothing to do, bored and sad. He exited the first set of doors and stood with the shopping carts looking out through the second set. Water running long in fast in all directions until finding the curb and joining the tumult, gushing towards the drains in dire unison. He watched and in his head heard them chanting, chanting, *we must die in this drain as one we must join the whole we must find the body we must be ONLY ONE or we will perish on the tips of flowers in the sun and disappear back into the clouds yes we must find the body or we are nothing.* A car pulled into an open spot and a girl jumped out and her hands and arms went up over her head as if the drops of rain were stones being thrown by angry boys. The flowers on her blouse sank onto her skin and her blue shorts darkened. Her feet in slippers, now like thin lace, he could see her toes as the first set of doors opened.

She looked up at him with a big grin on her face and her eyes wide.

"I guess it's raining out!"

"Is it?"

And she laughed and took a cart beside him.

"I'm just going to wait for it to stop."

"I think you are going to be waiting awhile."

"I'm very patient." That wasn't true.

"Good luck!"

She pushed her cart through the second set of doors and she was gone. *Jesus fucking Christ,* and he shook his head at her beauty and at her soft wet skin. *This sucks.* The second set of doors opened and he ran to his truck, keys in hand.

6.

(poem)

 i was starting to fall in love with this girl
that's a lie
i fell in love with this girl

she died
or might as well have

7.

(talks with men)

"Hey."

"What's up?"

"Nothing."

"Why are you laughing?"

"I saw that girl again."

"You did?"

"Yeah. Second date bro. Oh, and I got pulled over by the cops."

"For what?"

"Nothing. They thought I was lighting off fireworks. But that part doesn't really matter... man that girl..."

"I thought you didn't like her."

"I never said that. Anyway I like her now."

"What did you do?"

"Walked around the park for like three hours and then at the end we kissed."

"Nice."

"Dude, it was so weird."

"What?"

"Well, I just am so used to kissing in a certain way, you know? I haven't kissed anyone else in a long fucking time… No, it was a trip dude."

"Yeah?"

"Yeah."

"Was it a good kiss?"

"No."

One day I went to the beach. I hadn't been swimming in the ocean for about a year then. What a strange thing to do when you think about it. And I did think about it that day, watching all the people bobbing up and down in the waves with big smiles on their faces. I went to Rockaway. Have you ever been? I have never been to a beach with so many people. As far as I could see down the coastline were umbrellas and colorful bathing suits. This was also the first beach I'vebeen to with so many topless women. At the time I thought, *Is this a new thing I was not aware of? No one told me.* There were also kites and kids with buckets full of sand, couples making out in the water and people drinking beer from cans covered in those little beer cover things - *what are those even called?* - in order to not look like they are drinking beer but it just looks more like they are drinking beer. It was a strange beach too. The area used to be a naval yard. Or something. *The* whole place had huge empty brick buildings with boarded-up windows and roofs caving in and rusty equipment in their overgrown parking lots. I swam out pretty far and looked at my hands in the water and said to myself, *this is water,* in attempt to really connect with what I was doing. It was funny. But it made a difference. The whole thing was just... funny and enjoyable and odd at the time.

I went with our friend. The guy we used to call Neddy, even though that wasn't his name. I hadn't seen him in two years and he just happened to be in NYC when I was visiting. Neddy got in late the night before so I didn't see him until the morning. We are all staying our other friend's house who lived in NYC, the one we used to call Jrock, even though that wasn't his name either. Jrock had told me Neddy's mom had just died of cancer the week before. She'd had it for three years. In the morning I went for a bike ride and when I got back Neddy was up and Jrock was still sleeping. I almost said, "hey, I heard about your mom, I'm really sorry man," or something like that, but it just didn't happen. A couple hours later Jrock got up and he and his girlfriend went to Jersey so Neddy and I went to the beach, just the two of us. We drove in my truck about thirty minutes there, swam, lay on towels, and drove back. I never brought it up. And neither did he. We aren't so close that I could have just given him a hug right when I saw him and talked about it. But it felt odd not to talk about it at all. Really odd. I am sure he knew that I knew and of course I knew. So we both avoided this thing entirely for five hours. And now he's gone and I probably won't see him again for quite a while. There's something sad about that to me. Anyway, we didn't talk about you either. I know it's not the same thing. But you can't deny the poetic parallels.

9.

New York can be a sad place. New York can be a very sad place. New York can also be beautiful. But even it's beauty is shadowed in sadness. And that sadness is tied directly to being alone in the midst of 8.6 million people. Yes, there is something terrifically lonely about so many people moving together in the streets and in the subways, in the elevators and the stairwells, in the apartment buildings and the offices, in the grass in the parks and the concrete in the parks, doing everything possible to avoid eye contact and doing even more to avoid touch. Remember when we lived in Jersey City Heights for a couple years when you went to Law School at Rutgers? We took the train into New York sometimes and we would be pressed against strangers for 25 minutes. Our bodies intimately entangled butt to butt or groin to butt or groin to flank or face to face and the breath was all around us. The breath was hot and both rose above our heads and sank into our shoes and swam around us all as we were pinned to one another but refusing to acknowledge each-other's mere existence. Of course we held hands, you and I, and we acknowledged each-other, but we were engrossed in a social orgy where you keep your head down or stare off into space, where you turn up the music and put in your earbuds, where you zone out and pretend the presence of the other bodies has nothing to do with connection, it is merely a formality of NYC, on par with traffic noise or graffitti or gum on the sidewalk.

That night New York was a balloon of tepid air that sweats from leaves and stone. It's so hot people are dying in their buildings. The city has set up water stations and cooling stations because people are dropping like flies. He sees a dead man on the street covered in a sheet with four detectives in ties standing around him. On the bench near the man is a long cold cut sandwich still in plastic wrap and a coffee. He wonders if it is one of the detectives' or the dead man's. From under the sheet the dead man's stomach looks as wide as the corpse is long. He could see the dead man's shoes. He wants to ask, "did he die from the heat?" but they wouldn't tell him if he did. But he's pretty sure it was the heat that killed him and he thinks, *maybe the heat is going to kill us all*.

Later that night he goes out with friends who bring friends and they sit five in total. Two guys and three girls and one of his friends takes him aside and says in so many words, "yeah she's cute, she's sweet, she's smart, she's single, she's sitting there, in front of you, you are watching her." So he is watching her and she is talking and he is thinking, *yes, yes she is all these things* and *yes, I want to kiss her, I think.* He can imagine it. Kissing her. And she is talking about something and then he is talking about something and he is being funny and she is laughing but everyone is there and there's such a distance but he thinks he can see her looking at him when he looks away. Just like a brush stroke of water - you can't see it but if you run your hands down the paper, it's there and when you add color it sings. So he is doing the same. Brush strokes of water and he is giving them to her and hoping she knows but he doesn't know if she does.

She is drinking beer with Sprite. He is not drinking. She is drinking beer with Sprite and it is the cutest thing he can imagine. Beer with Sprite. She says, "and no one would even know I was drinking it. Maybe I'm not," she says and she is looking at him coyly and he is thinking, *yes, yes I could love her.*

So they leave and say goodbye and he gives her a high five just to connect with her once and so the sound of slap is there and they made it. He goes back to his friend's house and says, "yes, I like her. Give me her number."

And he sleeps. He doesn't dream.

In the morning he waits. It's so fucking hot and everyone is eating eggs and bacon and potatoes and he's just drinking water and wondering how anyone can eat in this fucking heat. And he's waiting. Then it is the afternoon and he calls but she doesn't answer so he leaves a message and sounds stupid because he's nervous. And he waits. Later she calls and he misses it because he's at the beach with a friend and he's swimming around and looking at his hands and saying, "you're in the water, you're in the water," and she leaves a message and she sounds sweet and answers his question - yes she'd like to do something. Soon they are on the phone talking briefly, and soon she is saying "so I will meet you outside at eight," and he is saying , "sounds good," and they hang up. And he waits.

He showers and sits in front of the fan and the fucking heat is everywhere and he's sweating as fast as the fan is spinning, in boxers with his legs up on the coffee table. No one is home and he's thinking about the salt water and the sand and the bare breasts, tanned and dark nipples and he's thinking, *try to kiss her, why not.* He is thinking about the water and his hands in the water and the way everything was moving in the water and thinking, *I am moving.*

It's eight o'clock and he sees her from the window walking down the street towards the apartment so he goes down.

11.

Her hands are small angels that hover around his and touch his face and take his face to her lips and she breathes into his mouth and the wet of her lips is on his in a night that is endless heat and dark light that is orange in the steam above a pond. They sit on a bench cradling each other's bodies like children. Like children in the middle of a park, in the middle of the city and there is no one there except the tiny licks of mosquitos that take blood from their legs as they take life from each other. She looks at his eyes and into his eyes and he looks at hers. Their noses touch their cheeks and she lets the straps of her dress fall from her shoulders and over her arms and she takes the buttons from his shirt one by one and weaves them through the small slits in the cotton and their chests are pressing against each other until the heart is beating against the heart that is beating and everything is warm. Everything is warm. And her breath is in his mouth.

And this goes on for four days and four nights until they find themselves at the ocean on a dark day of clouds and wind and the sea is rows of sharp edges and the water is thick with sand and seaweed and they are on towels in bathing suits cradling legs and arms and pressing heart to heart and tongues and eyes and it is here she is thinking, *yes I love him.* He knows this because that evening while naked she straddles him and sits there looking down at his face and touching his cheeks with her hands. They talk about what is happening and she says, "today I felt like telling you I love you." And they talk about this and later when the lights are off and he lays on her and they are kissing and holding, he moves his breath to her ear and says it. And she says it too, looking at his face in the dark until they are kissing again and holding. And later she cries for some time. And he tells her not to worry - "I'm coming back." And later he gets up and kisses her face and leaves her sleeping and takes a cab to the airport and gets on a plane. And later still, he is in a bed alone in California at his parents' house for a visit. A visit that is, maybe, supposed to assure his parents he is not dead either externally or internally. And he is alone for the first time in his parents' house since he was a child. And he is not dead. But he not entirely living in this moment. And he aches for her. And he aches for *her*. And he is wondering *Is this me? Am I here?* And of course it is and of course he is and he tries to sleep but the faces of women fly around him kissing him and leaving him and kissing him and leaving him until it is the morning and his eyes are red and he knows he fell asleep because he is thinking about a dream.

And time went on. And he did go back. And smelled the ways it did not fit. And besides, the first one is always a rebound they say.

12.

(letters to myself)

i feel lost. i feel like i lost something. where is it? what is it? and in this i feel helpless overwhelmed exhausted anxious ready and yet unready. circles circles circles. on the precipice or buried beneath it neither are safe.

13.

(poem)

i remember being asleep in the external process of
shedding you
i was so quiet

14.

Some nights I presumed myself dead. And I never awoke. Not really. I woke up and looked at things and I moved things around. I guess I progressed in one way or another but I never really accounted for it. I woke up and I looked to the right and the two windows there were clean cut squares with the shades drawn and I would know what time it was. Sometimes it was early evening and the cars were still going by outside, one every half hour. Sometimes it was in the earliest morning hours, black and silent and cold even when it was warm out and I would watch the window and the lack of movement and the still. And in that stillness I would feel the cascade building, building somewhere so far off it was a roar. And sometimes it was dawn, pale and pink and orange and sick and in that sickness of light from the window and the light from my chest, there was something like hope although I would never have described it that way at the time. I thought about you incessantly and without choice when the cars went by every half hour and when the death of night stopped the wind and when the pale, sick colors of dawn spread their legs over my face. I thought about you incessantly and without reason and without direction. And when I was riding shotgun in a work truck on the way to build a stone walkway, working for someone else for the first time in five years, and the nice chubby guy with the goatee and a wife and three kids asked about my separation I stopped him and I said, "I'll talk about anything else you want to talk about.

Just not that." And I looked out the window and was swallowed.

15.

(talks with you)

"I need to tell you something."

"You can tell me."

"I'm pregnant."

It was wet. The water hung in gray coats and clung to branches and seemed to come up from the earth when they walked. Up the hill behind the ramshackle collection of a dozen little six-by-ten co-op farm plots created by who, they never really knew. Maybe students from Amherst College. The plots were so different and so close together that at first glance it was just confusing to understand. One plot meticulously weeded and planted, with perfect rows that would take a straight edge to create, next to a plot with haphazard corn covered in Virginia creeper, next to a plot with weeds and a scarecrow built out of a shovel, a molding flannel, and a hat, next to a plot with rocks stacked tenderly together in a temple formation where a pair of sodden gloves were left askew on a ridge in the top stone, and on it went like that. Amethyst Brook running somewhere through the leaves and wood as they ascended the old logging trail. They talked about nothing. Nothing, that is, that either can remember, until they turned from the top and made their way back down and maybe time was seen then and maybe she took a breath and knew it was now or never and maybe she was terrified. They sat down on some rocks with lichen and some roots edged out of the earth for a moment and then stuffed their heads back down buried under their feet.

"I'm pregnant."

And everything that meant took years to understand because in that moment he just smiled and said something that in that moment was true and the absurdity of the ease to which that space took shape is baffling now and isn't it strange what is remembered most is the lichen on the rock and the way the roots dove into the earth.

17.

It just so happened that one of the last snows of the year began then. A snow that came when all other snow had melted and spring was sniffing around the edges of wood and lawns and river banks. The snow was bright and airy and floated in dry clumps, gentle as feathers, and the way it looked was beautiful on the roads of Massachusetts. And it just so happened this way in order to solidify the moment and the moments before and moments after in the silence of that last snow. That it didn't start until after they left the courthouse and after they hugged and after he got inside his truck and drove down the wide lanes of Greenfield and after he got on the highway and the road opened up and the trees pushed their heads into the gray is, in itself, a story of poems. Indeed, that the memory of the Northeast would only become one of nostalgia is a testament to that snow and even that day, when the heaviness should have broken the world. He drove away from everything he had known for over a decade, thinking of another woman and feeling the lightness of being completely alone with everything you own tied down in the bed of a truck and it is still morning and the gas in the tank has not even begun to drop.

18.

(three people)

"And this is mutual?"

"Yes."

"Yes."

"The big assets here are the two houses. You are both in agreement in the arrangements listed here?"

"Yes."

"Yes."

"Okay. And now we have this matter. What are you going to do about the child when they are born?"

"Uhm. Well..."

"It's not.. they're not...."

"Ah.... I see. The child is not of the marriage?"

"No, your honor."

"Okay. Well if there is nothing more we can close this out."

"No. Nothing more."

When she came back into the room she had washed
her face and without the dark eye makeup and the
hints of lip gloss and being naked as she was he fell in
love with her right then. She was a small and soft
animal, white and red and although she wasn't
shivering, he felt her this way. A doe or a fawn or
nymph or fairy or something that comes to you in a
dream of the forest when the weather is warm and
wet. When magic and depth is in the green and brown
and mist. She came to him and made a *meow* sound
and looked up at him. She came to him naked as she
was, not shivering but feeling that way and he was
with her then and it was perhaps the first meaningful
touch since New York and it was stronger because he
was stronger. It was deeper because he was opening.
It was safer, gentler, healthier because the blood was
dry and the wound was dressed. Yes. It was, in fact,
the first touch that wasn't in sickness or tracing
outlines or lost in shame or fear or desperate clutch.
He pressed his mouth against her mouth and neck and
ear and bones and hair and breast and held her and in
every moment inhaling breath. The smell of breath
and the smell of her. And maybe it was that night
when she fell in love with him or maybe it took her
longer. But that night they left their shoes at the door
and when they woke up in the morning they sat at the
kitchen with her housemate who shook his hand in
some sort of brotherly gesture of acceptance and
warning, nodding to the shoes with an air of
omnipotence as if to say, "I've known about your
presence before you presented yourself." She made

an omelet and said she wanted to stop eating meat. And at some point her housemate left and at some point she sat down on his lap and at some point he felt how they could do this or something like it forever. It was not terrifying. It was not elating. It was true. And it was simply a choice. And when, several months later, choice woke itself from slumber and came like a sulking bear to the river after months of winter, over the mountains of routine and safety and pattern that relationships erupt, carrying a question that must be answered like hunger after hibernation and moving with deft and unstoppable patience, he got on a plane to California and two weeks after that, got on a plane to Thailand. And although she held him to herself, open and accepting and bringing it all in before they said goodbye, she never spoke to him again.

Bangkok is a dark place when you carry darkness. You can stay at a hotel that is near the airport and is tall and narrow and wears itself like cheap perfume. Where most of the guests are there to bring back Thai girls and the others don't know that "visitors welcome" just means you can bring back Thai girls. You can leave the hotel by foot and you can walk the empty streets that zig zag perpendicular to the constant traffic of the highway at night and feel the heat from the packs of dogs that stalk you and stop and howl and fuck and stalk you again. Or you can hire a ride in a car with a thin man smoking and asking you, "where you from," and he will take you anywhere you want to go, with a little amulet hanging from the rearview mirror where his fox eyes stare at you hungrily. Or you can get on the back of a "death cab," a motorcycle with a young guy who doesn't wear a helmet but maybe has one for you and go full speed through halted traffic, weaving through bumpers and over sidewalks where your shin grazes a lamp post and you are sure you are going to die. And whatever direction you go you see the same things. You see trash and papaya trees in the sewage and water that canals along the streets. You see shops with garage doors open and men in bare feet squatted over a motor or soldering metal and a bed in the back of the shop where a child and mother are watching television. You see food vendors pushing carts and fruit sellers pushing carts and broom sellers pushing carts, always with a horn that sounds like a duck. You see the way the children watch you. You see the way they know something about you you do not know about yourself. And you see the beauty of a culture and a people consumed in a city like any other culture and people consumed in a city where life has become rough and hardened and fierce and desperate. And this is not a good representation of Thailand as a whole but it is Bangkok. And when you find yourself there with darkness in your pocket you look for the only salvation you can find. I can't say you would love it but I could see you walking around the streets and being pretty blown away. It's sort of like those streets we lived on in Jersey City Heights just a South-East-Asian-parallel-universe version.

There is so much I have never shared with you. Sometimes I forget what you know and what you don't. But I've shared this story with others many times. And I think of this time now with a smile and when I do share it with others it is often as something of a party favor. A good story that surprises and delights and draws the head to shake and the mouth to laugh. But the truth is, I needed her. And the time we shared together was quite serious for me. I didn't feel what I would describe as love but I did feel deeply present and connected and grateful and impassioned. And although I didn't feel what I would describe as love, I felt loved. And although I doubt she would say she loved me, I do imagine she felt tender and cared for and wanted. I imagine she too, felt loved. And this makes me think either I did, in fact, love her and she loved me or that love exists whether we would describe it that way or not. And, I suppose, it really doesn't matter that much.

I was at the bar. It was one block from my apartment in Florence near Northampton. It is the only bar I know of in Florence so I imagine you know the one I'm writing about. I walked there drunk by myself. I sat at the bar and ordered something I can't remember and I saw this woman in a black dress. Tall and white and slender and soft looking and I remember she was laughing and she came to the bar to order a drink and sort of fell and without thinking I reached for her and because I was already drunk I had a fire to me enough to say something like, "I've got you, beautiful." And that was pretty much all that needed to be said. She ordered something. We exchanged some sort of words full of tests and questions and calculations, all happening in the deep caverns of desire, memory, trauma; of lives full of confusion and mistake and pain and need. And because we were drunk we had the fire in us and I could see the way she looked at me was *wanting* and I was giving it to her so she knew I was wanting too. She went somewhere. Upstairs for a smoke, I think, where the bar opens up to the roof and you can bring your drink. I sat at the bar and ordered another one of whatever I was having. A couple sat down, all Carhartts and hill country, and I was drunk so I told them I was into this woman and that I was going to go find her. And they were smiling and telling me, "you got this." And maybe they were surprised when she came down the stairs and I reached for her. Surprised, perhaps, that she was twice my age or more. Surprised perhaps with the reverence in my voice and my gesture.

We went upstairs to smoke where the bar opens up. It opens up like a mouth and exhales you drunk into the fresh night and into the stars and the shock of clean air is sobering in a way that does not pull the fire from you. And I leaned into her and into her height that started half a head above me and into her black dress and she fell back into her heels against the wood railing and I kissed her with more passion than I had ever kissed another human being in my life because the fire was hot and because my life had brought me here slaughtered and born and I would create everything I would need for life to continue and if I didn't do that in every fucking moment, I would perish.

We came down from the bar and someone said, "I just want you to know we can see everything up there on these video cameras," and gestured to a TV behind the bar and they said it in some way as to evoke shame and I felt nothing but good and I shrugged. I paid. Maybe I paid for her too, I don't know. And we walked back to my apartment and she leaned on me and there was no mistake, she was shivering.

And in the morning I looked at the two windows that were clean cut squares with the shades drawn and I knew that it was dawn and sickness was softer and I woke her up and made love to her again. After, I drove her home in my diesel Cummins flatbed. It was a few blocks from town. She had me drop her off halfway down the road from her house. Her mom was visiting or her sister or something. "I don't want to get any shit from them," she said and climbed out of the truck but before she did, I reached for her face and I kissed her. And maybe that was when I noticed that her teeth were too straight and too white to be hers and that her skin was long and that her eyes were sad with age. But I didn't think anything more about it. It was just a noticing. I thought she was beautiful, really. Hungover and tender and needing me to drop her down the street like a highschooler that snuck out of the house. It was sweet. I also know my heart was an open wound and I could feel the blood in my shoes and later that day I felt a deep regret and sorrow. Not because I felt ashamed of who I had chosen to share my body with for the first time since our separation. But because I thought there was a possibility that we might get back together then and I thought maybe I had really fucked it up. Not knowing you would be pregnant with someone else's child a month or two later.

22.

(talks with men)

"She's going to be there tomorrow."

"Holy shit. I haven't seen her in like eight years."

"Just..."

"What?"

"Be cool, you know?"

"What do you mean?"

"I don't know."

"I'm cool. I can handle it dude, don't worry about it."

"Okay."

"I've been in love with her since I was fourteen, man. It makes sense I'm excited to see her."

"I know. That's what I mean though."

"It's cool. I'll be chill, dude. I can handle it."

"Okay."

23.

(poem)

after removing her clothes and the shades from the
light and the coins from her eyes

24.

The ocean in Santa Cruz is ugly. Have you been there? I don't think you have. It is ugly but not in the way that it lacks beauty. It is ugly in the way that it takes you in and pushes you out. In the way that the rocks stick their gross bodies into the sea from all angles and some even roll back and forth and forward and back with the push and pull of the surf. In the way that the day can be flat and sun-filled on the bluff and when you reach the shore it will turn dark and suffocating and the surface of the sea swells with white caps like a painting held over a flame, beginning to splinter and open up and fall away. In the way the sea is always moving in chaotic undecipherable patterns. In the way the sea is always agitated. In the way the sea has rough hands and both wants you and repels you. In the way you can sit and watch her move and fall into her deeply entranced and overtaken and when you get close you can feel her cool dragon breath and the way she can kill you and decide to take you into her womb or leave you on the shore.

25.

(poem)

if i were to come over to your house tonight
would you be the grizzled armor of wings and the
baron of axes or all lips and tongue and honeysuckle

26.

(letter to her)

I had a hard time falling asleep but when I did I slept deep and hard and dreamed crazy and woke up with crusties in my eyes. I am anxious about the future. My life is going to look so different so quickly. Today I am helping her fix a few things here in Turners Falls. Then I am going to go to Belchertown in the evening. Tomorrow I will pack up my truck. The next day I get a divorce, get in my packed Ford, and head west. I am excited for the new changes but also feeling something hard to describe. A feeling of a new life truly coming to light. I feel that for the last year I have been unfolding and soon that will stop and I will look around and I will have a new home, a new color, a new smell. Not that the process of change itself will end but that *this* one will.

Anyway. I am, of course, thinking a lot about you. I want to be able to touch you when I talk. I hope you have a wonderful and productive day. I will give you a call when I head down to Btown.

-c

He was awake and could smell the still, morning ocean in the breeze that moved the light, white curtains like a dream over the window. A cat raised its head from its black body and yawned pushing a paw out and then pulling it back and covering its head to sleep again, curled between his legs. Tiny figurines stared at him from a shelf on the opposite wall, their porcelain eyes painted blue. The fake flowers in the large glass vase on the table rustled lifeless in the breeze that now was picking up, flowing across his face like a soft hand, graceful and with some force.

He pulled the white sheet and heavy white woven cover from his naked body. The cat lifted its head toward him with eyes closed, just for a moment, before tucking it back into its black body. Standing, he looked into the mirror that hung on the white door. He looked at his brown skin and thin black hairs on his chest. He looked at his penis, curled like a soft hairless mouse, and his balls, warm and heavy like fresh laid eggs. He looked at his face. Dark circles puffed around his eyes and white skin with red blotches like splatters of paint across his cheeks and down his neck. He looked at his eyes. Those sad, sad eyes. Brown and green and red and pinched and wet. He stayed that way for some time until a long breeze swam over his lips and under his nose and that still, morning ocean smell filled a breath that reached deeply internal and called something.

He dressed and went downstairs, opened the large white door where the stained glass was beginning to sparkle under the light of the rising sun and walked down to the dock across the street. He took the short path of dead grass and green sprigs of something attempting to create life in a warmer than usual winter and failing, curled back on themselves. The crushed stone compacted and moved under each step. The dock was long and narrow and chunks of it had been pulled for the winter, tied with red and blue rope to the sides of the large piers poking up from the water like erections, making the thin walkway thinner so he had to turn sideways to get past. He walked to the end of the dock and sat down with his legs dangling over the edge. If he stretched he could dip a toe in the black water. He looked out over the ocean and the sun that sat atop it, a bright orange orb glittering and he thought about last night.

The phone had rung in his ear again. Voicemail picked up.

"Babe. It's me. Again." He was pacing. "Fucking a, call me back." He hung up and sat down on the couch turning on the volume on the television. The Patriots got a touchdown. He watched the screen without really watching it and reached down for the bottle without really looking for it. He took a long pull from the whisky, then chased it with a beer he'd stuffed between the couch cushions earlier.. A drop of whiskey rolled from his lip and down the cleft in his chin and continued rolling down his neck over his Adam's apple and onto his bare chest. He was still holding both the bottles and thinking about doing it again when the phone rang.

"Hello."

"Hey sorry."

"I've called you like ten times."

"I know I was... I left my phone. I'm sorry."

"You know I hate that shit." He was pacing in front of the white painted brick fireplace with the mantle and fake flowers in glass cases and that tiny sailboat centered below the glass mirror that reflected pale yellow light and flashes from the television screen.

"I'm sorry."

He sighed and stopped pacing and sat back down on the couch. "When are you coming back?" He pulled the beer from the cushions and drank.

She was quiet.

"Babe?"

"I'm... Well... Today they offered me a leadership position and the pay is almost double."

He felt his blood get hot. He was staring at the television but the screen just blinked colors. "So. What does that mean?"

"I'm going to stay longer."

He propped the phone between his head and shoulder and took up the whiskey and drank quickly chasing it with the beer. He put the whiskey back down and drank the beer again. "How long?"

"I don't know."

"This was supposed to be two weeks. It's been two months. How much longer are you going to stay?" He could feel anger like a sharp stone in his gut and sadness from its weight.

Nothing was really said after that. They said, "I love you" out of habit and in a way that expressed passive distaste and anger and despair and frustration on both ends. Then they hung up.

He kept pulling from the whiskey until it was empty and he laid down in a bed that wasn't his own with sheets and pillows that weren't his own. He could feel the porcelain figurines staring at him from the other room. The black cat jumped up on the bed and he pulled her warm body close to himself. She pulled herself away and walked to the end of the bed, curled up, and went to sleep. He lay there for hours and at some time the night took him in and he did not dream.

The next day he sat on the dock at the end of the road. He saw the island across the channel, empty. He saw the docks poking out from the shorelines full of moored canoes and kayaks. He saw the houses shut tight, some with painted plywood over the windows, some with burlap wrapped around young evergreens and rhododendrons, some with leaves piling up in corners of hedge lines where the wind couldn't get through. And he saw the silence and the abandonment and the death of it all. And he said out loud or maybe to the island or maybe to the now smooth, small rock in his belly, "what the fuck am I doing here?" But he didn't move.

He didn't move for some time.

Cape Cod during the winter is for those who cannot leave. It is not a treasure trove of winter work or someplace to start or grow a business like we thought it would be. Although I am not sure you ever really thought that. Maybe it was all my idea and you just nodded your head and waited for your exit to reveal itself. Or maybe you were fighting, really hard, to believe something your whole being was denying. Maybe a little bit of both. I can tell you, it was a strange time for me and I've never wanted to go back, be it winter or summer. I think I saw too much or maybe I created too much. Everything was the underbelly. The inside out. The upside down. It was all the things we could not see when we visited a couple times in the summer and in the early fall before the place really clears out and shows its darkness.

One day I walked to the bus stop because the big diesel Cummins needed something and was at the mechanic. We had left the Ford in Belchertown, unregistered, to bear the winter alone. I needed booze or food or something that equated to nothing at all. I walked down the road and this girl came out of her house and waved and smiled at me. All white and small and young and skinny and her teeth were there, pushing forward in a mix of attractive and off-putting. I could tell right away she had a sickness. Most of them do have a sickness. The ones that live here year-round. And most often for the young-ones it's pills or it's h.

Maybe I waved back. I'm sure I did. But I felt confused at her vigor. I crossed the street and sat down on the bench at the bus stop. She followed me. She was wearing sweatpants and a sweatshirt both extra large and hanging limply on her tiny frame and she had just her finger tips out of the sleeves, curled down on her palms to clutch the cuff of the sweatshirt to keep the winter out. She crossed the street and sat down on the bench near me. I could see the sick on her face and the way it brings a shade with it that is like no other color and the way it pulls down on the eyes from the inside and the way it pushes small patches of red and blemish and rash from the neck line. And I could see that she was young. And I could see that she was frail. And I could see that she was looking for something. . Anticipating. She was waiting too, just in a different way than me.

"Hey."

"Hey."

"Are you taking the bus?"

"Yeah."

"Oh. Okay."

And she got up and left. It took me a while to figure out what had just happened. And I could be wrong. But I'm pretty sure she mistook me for a John. Not a dealer because she would know a dealer. But a John she had made some arrangement with to meet around that place at around that time. And I could feel the way she was ready to be with me. And I could feel the way parts of me woke up like wolves wake up with hunger from the smell of warm blood. And given that I was one of the only humans around and that I was male and that I was sad and hunched over and that I probably smelled of need, it made sense she would assume I was the one, even if I crossed the street and sat at the bus stop. I saw her a few times after that walking around expecting and anticipating and ready and sick and always drowning in that extra large sweatshirt.

Cape Cod during winter is empty and sad and carved-out and stark and naked. I lived there for ten weeks and waited for you every day in a rented summer house full of someone else's knick-knacks. I had one neighbor on a street of otherwise empty, well-cared-for, single-family homes with little yards, all with access to a shared dock. My neighbor was lonely and he stank of it as much as I did. He lived with his ninety-year-old mother. His greatest expression of life was going to kite fairs and flying kites. We would chat sometimes when I was cleaning out my truck and he was pretending to do something in the front yard just to be able to hear the sound of his own voice and know that someone else heard it too. I drank everyday and I took what pills I could find and I worked on empty homes in strange, cold inlets and cul-de-sacs and I waited.

I started watching football because it was the only way I could be in a bar by myself and feel like I wasn't alone and that I was part of some collective. I would express myself when the Patriots missed a touchdown or made one because I wanted to hear the sound of my own voice and know that someone else heard it too. And the winter grew and collapsed and grew again between sun and gray and snow and snowmelt and I waited. Everyday I waited.

Until I couldn't wait anymore. And I left parts of my skeleton on the shore and in that bed and maybe in one of those cold, dark houses where I cleaned up an abandoned refrigerator or blew out the lines of already cracked copper tubing, too late to save a damn thing. I took what bones I could back to a new apartment in Florence and you were going to move in with me the next day. But instead we sat on a mattress I dropped in one of the bedrooms and I asked you if you needed to leave and you said you did. And that was it.

29.

(poem)

so the Quabbin gave way to a sea
and blueberries and soil-handed women are a shade
beneath the maples that i smell
not on the sand and not on the palm trees
but in my bed when i sleep

Belchertown, Massachusetts is a simple place. But it has secrets. We discovered them together because we lived there and we let the place slowly become us. One such secret: changing its name from Cold Spring to Belcher's Town in an act of homage to the then governor. Another: burying the broken bodies of the mentally disabled in the late nineteenth and early twentieth century in a mass unmarked grave from the now abandoned mental institution. The one we used to drive through just to look at. The entrance is right off the main road, all brick and square and boarded up with tall grass and untold horror. The grave site has since been marked in restitution and acknowledgment of the town's crime but there is no clear path to it and no one would know it exists right behind the soccer field of the high school unless you're a high schooler who sneaks off between classes to smoke pot or you have, as we did, a habit of walking your dogs on narrow trails that litter Route 22.

Nonetheless, Belchertown is a simple place where Route 22, 202, and 9 all intersect and overlap just for a moment to show visitors the three pizza places, the Dunkin Donuts, the Subway, the two Chinese restaurants, Ace Hardware, Stop-n-Shop, and Checker's Market, with the addition of a couple liquor stores, of course. The Quabbin reservoir sits neatly at the edge of the north border. A beautiful and still, haunting, silent body of water that, rumor has it, on a particularly clear day when the light is just right you can take a boat into the middle and see the top of a church steeple buried deeply below the blue and black and yellow of the water. The Quabbin drowned a few hamlets when it was created. It now provides water for Boston. No one can swim in it unless they want a fifty thousand dollar fine but you can take a gas boat out and fish it and put the guts of the fish back in. We just parked at one of the few dozen hidden entrances at the ends of roads or tucked away off Route 202 and Route 9 with heavy, locked, yellow gates and walked in beyond the tree line just to take in what a vast, man-made body of water looks like and how empty and alone it must be feeding a city over a hundred miles to the East and bathing the empty bones of hamlets in her belly.

To understand you have to go back to age fourteen. To really understand you have to go back to childhood and what a mother means and what a womb is and what a man is not and that is too much. But you can go back to age fourteen when the first touch came to be. When she took him by the hand and pulled him across the street away from their friends and into the pea fields that ran along the road outside of Dunn School in Los Olivos, California with thin, string lines running back and forth in rows four or five feet high and full and dense as clay walls with the wild, winding of pea shoots, their pregnant pods hanging from every direction, bursting and swollen. She took him into those walls and laid him down and climbed on top of him and took off her shirt and took off his shirt and kissed him for hours. He put her breast in his mouth and felt a couple stray hairs around the areola and nothing has remained as strong as that memory. The way that soft small breast took shape in his mouth and the contrast of and realness of those two stray hairs that, in later years when they lay together again in her bed in Santa Cruz, he never told her about but always looked for and never found. And in those fields a mother and a child were born and they played out their sadness together in downtrodden ways for the next decade when stars aligned themselves just so. And it is impossible to know what was born for her and what she carried and what she felt and if the fields possessed her like they possessed him. But for him those hours were all young flesh and warmth and smell and ache and love and overflow and capsize and crawl back in. It was a storm. It was a moment that changed his life and for all the wind and hail and fire and fury he walked through, he could never shake it from himself. And some time after that it happened again but with a different girl and the meaning was different and the feeling was different and the kissing and the breasts and the skin were different. But the depth was the same and the way the peapods hung and quietly watched, that was the same too.

32.

(letters to myself)

I.

there isn't any way i can stay in this state

kind of feel like shit. but I'm also drunk. four beers sixteen oz nine percent. talked to my friend tonight. thought I was helping him but ultimately feel like I didn't. feel judged. probably me judging myself? he doesn't want advice just wants someone to listen I'm thinking… still want to drink more even though i am pretty smashed at three PM. still feeling fat. making a collage.

being drunk feels like a dream--- acts like a dream.

II.

i am remembering my dream from last night. haunting. gross. dirty. i was in a foreclosure. going to change a lock. the neighbors were white ghetto poor underclass impoverished foul-mouthed dirty and drunk. i saw something horrible and i could not stop it. then i woke up or the dream changed i don't remember. but i dream about those foreclosures a lot.

it is my most common dream by far. and it often has the same feeling. sad heavy dirty. it feels like life sometimes. well. internal life that is. my emotional world sometimes feels like those dirty broken dark sad foreclosures. that is an intense metaphor. i don't feel sad about this.

III.

mm i liked her belly though. i could use a momma body to cuddle with right now. well. maybe not right now. i feel pretty absorbed with being alone. but i could use it. just. around. when i wanted it. Thailand. will i have a Thai partner? maybe... just maybe. would have to be the right girl but... i could definitely see it. god Thai girls are beautiful that is for sure.

Pai is cold at night in the winter months. Don't let them tell you you don't need a jacket in Thailand. If you go to the mountains and if you go in winter, you will find your breath in the dark night and you will sit closer to the fire outside your bungalow and you will search for a body to press against your body. And when you go dancing you will not want to leave. And you will drink Sangsom and eat Thai chili and garlic to keep stoked the fire in your belly. And you will find that if you sleep alone you will pull the blankets up around your head. And you will find if you don't sleep alone you bury yourself in another body. I did. And I took her round, white body and lost myself in the folds of her belly and slept like a baby on a breast sucking the milk of her scent and skin, resting my hand on the mound of her blonde pubic hair until dawn crept over the trees and bathed roofs and grass and river in warmth and everything opened up and exhales. I doubt it would be just like that for you but I do imagine you may find your own version whether you remember to pack a jacket or not.

34.

(poem)

re: drugs
i am not a prisoner i am a patient

The last time I smoked oxy was with you. It was after you slept somewhere else. After I went back to the Cape and packed everything up. After I dropped the mattress on the floor in Florence. But it was before I asked you if you needed to go and you said you did. I think the oxy gave me the courage to ask and gave you the courage to answer.

Remember, I was pissed at you for getting it. I asked to see it. I threw it out the window. We went to a hotel. It rained. I found texts on your phone to another man. I left. I came back the next day from the Cape and said, "let's go find that pill." And we did. It was wet but intact, just sitting there in a parking lot in Northampton. Eighty milligrams. Blue. We made a square of aluminum foil and took the guts out of a pen. We held the lighter under the foil and watched the pill run like a droplet with a trail of black behind it and took in that smoke to fill the gaps in our breaking hearts. There is not a way to write about it without dramatic obscenity. There is no way to make it softer. There is no way to make it pretty. It just was what it was.

Relief.

It was Christmas Eve in the Santa Ynez valley. It was evening and that means that it was cool and fresh and dark out. It means that the stars were clear and floating in the blue-black of sky. It means fewer cars were out and fewer shops were open as he drove down the gentle curve of Main Street before it T's and looks out over the sleeping fields just beyond a thin barbed wire fence. Fields that caught fire one year and was the most exciting thing that happened in quite a while. The smoke curled up into the sky in a gentle dance and the thin fire gripped the brown grass in desperation, burning faster than it could spread on a windless day. It went out on its own or maybe with a little help but either way it merely left a patch of black earth that grew back the following year and was forgotten.

At the bottom of the curve before the T, he turned left into the parking lot thinking the words "be cool" and parked. The Maverick Saloon sat behind him lit in yellow light. It looked like something out of a Hollywood western but it wasn't. It was stock SYV, as original as the ranchers and the cows themselves. Not as original as the Chumash or the poppies but certainly more original than grape arbors and boutiques. The front was weathered wood held together in long lateral lengths with a short deck and a door that was propped open. Someone was smoking under the eaves and the light coming from the doorway was orange.

He got out of the car and walked up the steps. The person smoking looked at him and nodded, his cowboy hat tipping down and his eyes lost in shadow. He went inside.

The ceiling of the Maverick Saloon is covered in dollar bills and the occasional bra and panties. How this began and how it continues is a question for someone else. But the effect is uncomfortable, contrasting obscurely with the large boxy wooden bar and dark plank flooring and brown walls. Nonetheless it is classic SYV and the only bar in town and it was open on Christmas Eve and it was where they said they would meet and so he walked inside and found them at a booth in the front room just beyond the bar.

"There he is." The biggest one stood up to hug him. There were five of them total, all friends from high school or even before, all with stories and assumptions and memories that were one-sided and sweetly nestled in childhood where they walked the streets of Buellton at night with nothing to do or listened to Man is the Bastard and sewed punk rock patches onto their clothes with dental floss or took long rides in cars smoking pot down Refugio Road where it criss-crossed over Quiota Creek or where they cried together because youth is painful and it doesn't matter where you live or what color you are or what sort of parents you have, it just hurts sometimes. And between two of them on one side of the booth, there she was and although she had grown and although she had on clothes and although she was sitting at that booth, he saw her nestled sweetly in childhood where memory is one sided and pea pods are hanging from her hair and she is naked and her breasts are small and her hands are on his face and her eyes are in his stomach.

The night unfurled itself as it always does until he found himself alone with her talking at the bar. She ordered hot water and that's all because she said, "cold water is shocking to the system and you should always drink water warm," and she gave him the mug to sip from. She smelled of alcohol and breath and when they stood at the bar he took in everything he could as she looked down at her shoes that were black and tightly laced as she played between coy and shy and solid and open and just distant enough to leave a man second guessing himself.

He told her about his wife and she told him about her fiancé and they laughed about the fact that they were both left around the same time and were now here in life dropped off like children on a street in some new world and about to find their way with both tears and light in their eyes.

He wasn't drinking and when his friend needed to go, he told her to come with him. He drove his friend home and then took her back to the bar. They sat in the car in the parking lot and he took her hand and asked to kiss her. And she dipped her head and he smelled her breath and she said she was still feeling a lot or something like that and it was too soon or something like that. And he was being cool so he said he understood and he'd like to stay in touch.

He saw her a couple more times that week with friends. Then he went to the airport and flew to Bangkok. On the flight he kept thinking of her shoes in the bar and the mug of hot water and the way when, in the car he had asked for a kiss and she dipped her head, her hair looked like smoke curling up in a gentle dance and looking back, he could see how the fire between them burned too fast to take hold and how the lack of movement in the air just left a black patch on the earth that eventually grew back and you had to look really hard to find the ashes.

37.

(poem)

a body is the soft part of the world we find when we
are lonely

(talks with men)

"Come on have a drink with me."

"Nah man. I've got this huge flight."

"Exactly. Come on. When am I even going to see you again? You're going to go to Thailand to disappear or die or something."

"Okay."

They met up in Solvang, California at around one PM and ordered a beer. The first he had had in some time. They drank two pints together.

"So what are you going to do over there?"

"Just get out of my head I guess. Eat some fruit. Travel around."

"Well... I think it will be good for you man."

"Yeah. Me too. It will be good... I am thinking a lot about her though. I mean. Isn't it weird that we both broke up with our people at the same time? It just seems like... I don't know..."

"Man. I don't know. I think you need to let that go. She's... you know.."

"Dangerous?"

"Sorta. Yeah. Something like that. I've known her for a long time man and I don't really trust her and it's not that she's not great. She's great. But... I just wouldn't take that all on right now."

"Yeah."

"And I think you're sort of obsessed with her."

"I know... it's just... it is weird right? It seems like we just keep coming back into each other's lives."

"Hey. Maybe it's meant to be. I don't fucking know man. I just think you should be careful. Like. Slow. Or something."

"Yeah... thing is... I'm pretty fucking lonely dude."

"Yeah... thing is... I'm pretty fucking lonely dude."

He didn't say this last part out loud. He just thought it and they started talking about something else and they finished their beers. They hugged a deep hug with years of friendship between them and left the bar. It was two PM in Solvang, California. The sun bounced around the soft, earthy, red tile roofs and white washed walls of Main Street as tourists wandered around in polos with cameras. Across the street there was a Danish pastry shop and an ice cream parlor and few stores that sold knick-knacks and figurines with piercing eyes just like the ones on the Cape and he remembered walking through those stores when he was twelve and pocketing a little jewelry case with a mirror bottom that later he used to store weed and later he used to store pills. Further down the main street he could see the Peterson Inn where he used to work when he was fourteen serving those same Danish pastries, bagels, eggs and coffee to old white couples that read the newspaper in silence and left him dollar bills that he accumulated to buy weed and then later, pills.

A car pulled up and he got inside and it took him to the airport. At the airport he found a bar and ordered another beer. On the plane, he ordered a couple more. Then he was in Taipei for a long layover and it was morning there. He walked to a park and saw old men moving in rhythm, twisting one direction then the other slowly, slowly letting their arms flail against their bodies. It was cold. The sun was moving up in the sky. He found a bar and drank a beer and drank another. He walked around a mall where two girls with straight, shining black hair and white socks and black shoes and skirts turned around to look at him and laugh. He walked past a billboard of Brad Pitt lounging in white clothes with a large beard and he thought about his own large beard and that maybe it wasn't as strange here as he'd thought. Maybe those girls were just flirting and that's how it was done here. Maybe they weren't laughing at him at all.

He made it back to the airport. The beer, the lack of sleep, the time warp of traveling over half the world, all coming together with overwhelming weight and he found the gate for his next flight and asked someone to wake him up when the flight was boarding and he fell asleep thinking of those girls and his beard and his friend and how bizarre it all was.

Someone woke him up. He got on the plane. He slept. He woke up as the plane touched down in Bangkok. He found a driver and showed him the address of a hotel in Thai and in fifteen minutes he was there in the middle of concrete and cars and roads and there was something industrial and dirty about it all. He found his hotel hiding itself in fuchsia and two pots overflowing with tropical plants at the doorway, and there was a tiny-framed doorman, swimming in a dark red, worn suit with a cap and he opened the door for him and took his bags and made big eyes when he gave him a US dollar.

Up in his room he fell asleep. Time was abstract. It was dark out and when he woke up it was dark out. The consciousness of his loneliness evaded him but sat on the bed like a tired lover fading into the backdrop of movement and breath and thought. Just there. He ate some of the things in the fridge. He drank water.

He felt a darkness in his pockets.

Five minutes later he was downstairs, outside, climbing into a car with a thin man smoking a cigarette. He asked him if he'd go to Soi Cowboy.

"I take you anywhere you want to go."

40.

(letters to myself)

I.

This bed is so comfortable. This house is so cozy. When it's dark there are small lights on in the kitchen and there are Christmas lights on outside, and they shine in through the windows, so even in the darkness there is light and it is a dim, red-orange light. You walk on the carpet in bare feet and feel the blast of hot air from the ceiling vents on your way to the bathroom and it just feels so loving.

I know this place so well. The carpet is new and things have moved around a bit, the walls are painted fresh and my room is now full of sewing machines and quilts my mother makes. But I still know the bones of this house like my own. I can still traverse its rooms and hallways, my eyes barely open, only in underwear and fully comfortable.

But now I am asleep. It's four in the morning and somewhere just outside of consciousness there is a tiny fan buzzing that my parents bought and set up days before my arrival because they know I like white noise. During these early morning hours, I dream. I dream my ex-wife is not pregnant and that she is not my ex-wife at all. I am changing the sheets on the bed and she is lying on the bed and it is then I see she has a paper plate out with two large lines on it and a pen with guts taken out in her hand. She is caught but she smiles and says "come on." And she snorts one of the lines. I can't believe she is doing this to me. "What are you doing?" She is smiling like it is nothing. I have to leave. I feel myself wanting to stay and do drugs with her and fuck her on the bed, high as shit and warm. But I have to leave. I tell her so.

She doesn't resist, just smiles but I can see her pain. She knows she is wrong and she takes up the other line. I leave the house we are in, which is horribly slanted. I feel fear and sadness and I am searching for my ex-girlfriend who is still my ex-girlfriend in the dream. She has just dyed her hair orange, which was also real. It is longer in the dream and it covers her soft, white face beautifully. She is in a bathtub fully clothed. I take her hand, I have something serious I need to ask her. I am going to ask her to marry me but she starts telling me a story and we become different people. I am now a prisoner, trapped in an old brick prison with a group of other prisoners, awaiting death as rain begins to push through the walls and fills up the basement room where we are huddled. There are maybe twenty of us; men, women, children. The water is coming in everywhere in thick, aggressive drops. Someone breaks down a door and we run up the stairs, break down another door, and we are out of the prison and into the woods. We have become animals. There are bears and deer and squirrels and I am a red woodpecker and so is my ex-girlfriend who is not my ex-girlfriend but just a bird, and she is flying with me. There are three of us - is the third my ex-wife? As we fly through the woods one of us is attacked by a hawk and gets away and -

I wake up.

II.

I woke up this morning and know I dreamed about my ex-girlfriend again. I can't remember the dream now. It's been too long. It's dark now and I am waiting to go see some old friends. Some people I haven't seen in a long time. And a girl. Maybe. Yeah. I can't even think about her right now since I have thought about her off and on since I was fourteen. Sometimes with such a craving I felt I really had no control. Other times just like - what the fuck? You know. Why is this girl stuck in my mind. I've written poetry about her. And I learned to touch a girl's face while kissing from her, because that's how she kissed mine. And kissed my ears and neck and held my lips. God. Nothing like that have I ever experienced again. Yeah. Her. She may come. She may. So my friend says. He thinks I'm obsessed with her. Fuck him. I don't think "obsessed" is the right word at all. Obsessed implies an issue, a problem. She's... a dream. I dream about her. She's my go-to dream girl. So what. I have no real designs of her or this night. It is doubtful she will show. But the fact she said she might tells me she is single. I don't think she knows I will be there. I am not saying she is coming for me. But this bar is a piece of shit and we who are going are almost all men and all lost and all looking and needing and... and she may walk in and I may be there with my big beard and look at her and she will know I've been waiting. Everyone else will be drunk and drinking and making fools of themselves and their bodies will be smelling like the first snows of death and there I am. Waiting and rosy-cheeked, strong under my garments and showing clarity through my eyes and smelling like rosemary tea. You never know. She might turn up and we might go home together. She might show up and we might not go home together. She might not show at all. I don't know. If she doesn't show I will still wonder about her. If she does show, that dream may die. Or it may get stronger and kill me in some lonesome state in Thailand. As it almost killed my marriage seven years ago when she came onto me and we made out like children in a tent next to my passed out friend who knew nothing about it until yesterday. The same friend who thinks I'm obsessed. He doesn't know shit about it. And come on. He knows me. Obsessed is not the right word at all. She just comes and goes. For a time I thought about her endlessly. And for a time I didn't think of her at all. I hope I see her. Just to see her. To update my dreams. She is still twenty-one when I think of her. Hopefully she is fat and has no teeth. I could let her go. No. I don't want to let her go. I like having her around. I wonder what would happen if we made love. I think I would die. There would be nothing else in the world to accomplish, to see, to touch, to taste, to smell, to hold. Nothing. She is some wondrous creature. If you have ever known something like this, you only think you have known something like this.

III.

Last night was dark up the mountain above Santa Barbara. I went up with my friend who lives there now. I haven't seen him in a long time. We were driving up the road on S curves in his old Dodge, the rock wall on one side, a sharp angle of shale stone I'm sure is ready to lie down in front of us at anytime.

Up on the mountain things are different. People give a shit. People are quiet. And people talk calmly and laugh easily. No problem. Sit down. Wherever you want. Pet the dog. Up the mountain. Old trucks that don't move and piles of rotting wood and heaps of tires. Everything is there for a goddamn reason and everything has a goddamn purpose but nothing matters all that much and the wind blows different up there.

"You can move up here after Thailand," my friend says. And I think I might. Or stay down in town and rent the studio apartment from my parents' rental property. The same house I lived in until I was three with the big avocado tree and the bamboo.

By the time we arrive the rain has started and it is dark. My friend checks on the chickens. One extra - "Hmm. That's weird. Someone else threw their chicken in with mine." He closes the cage. We put some wood in a wheelbarrow and I push it up the hill. He stacks it in the stove and lights it with a blowtorch and we go to tell the sisters that the sauna is lit. He knocks on the door and we hear guitars stop and he opens the door and it's all hellos and this is me and sit wherever and talk like I know you and there are two of them and one is chubby and has two kids and the other is tall and lean and a bit fierce and quite a beauty, brunette and dominant in her movements, she is one graceful gesture of strength, and the third, the third is not there. *Maybe I will meet her later*, I think. He thinks I should work on the fierce one. He thinks I can get her tonight, he says, "no problem." Whenever some guy tells you this, you know they are lying. And I do. But later I cut my fingernails, just in case.

So we go to the sauna and strip down and lay out and just sweat man. We just sweat and talk kinda quiet about what, I forget now. And then go stand in the rain, our cocks just hot with sauna, and our balls don't shrink a bit out there just standing in the cold ass rain. Waiting for the sisters, you know. We have to stick it out for the sisters. My friend has a girlfriend. A quiet, blond girl and I think he loves her but I think he also wants attention from other women. I can understand that. Well, it's some time later and we've been in and out and in and out and we are out in the rain, ass naked, arms crossed under the dripping overhang of rotten wood and the rain-mist, tickling our cocks and here she comes, the fierce one, and she is with a guy and her headlight flashes on me and I know she checks my body out to see what it looks like. *Not bad,* she thinks, I think. And the guy with her I don't worry about. Nothing happening with this chick right now. "Lay the groundwork," now my friend is saying. See how it changes. So I get back in and sit down and she is already naked and the candle my friend lit when we first arrived is dim now to the point I can only see her pussy is hairy. And I like it like that. And I can see her breasts and they look firm, yes, nice. But

I can't really see them. Just enough to know, yes, nice. And so what this other guy is here. I'm not worried about it.

She pulls the albacore shell out of the water bucket and a few times pours the water on the rocks until the steam burns our faces. I can smell her vagina. There is no question. I can smell her. She smells like brine and soil, a sexy vagina, hairy. My face gets lost in it. That smell is intoxicating and strong, man. It fills the room and is inside the steam so I am covered in it. My friend is dying so he's out and I'm leaving too. "Have a good night." Groundwork. We pass by the house later in the evening and the third sister is about. She has a kid. I like her the most. Maybe because she seems a bit softer. A bit. Easier to hold maybe. "Hi", "hi", "it's nice to meet you", "goodnight". You know. Quick. I like her. Maybe. Next time, next time.

Yeah so I go to sleep and I dream about girls and my ex-girlfriend is there. She would have loved it up on the mountain. I could have held her in my arms in that sleeping bag they let me use with that wood stove blazing so hot we had to open a window and the rain just falling all night and she wouldn't mind me getting up to pee in the dry river bed. She wouldn't mind at all. Just turn her head up to me and say quietly, "meow." This image is the saddest thing in the fucking world.

It's later in the night now, the next day. Just waiting to go see these friends at the Maverick. Most are idiots. And he texts me, "the sisters think you're really cute." What does this mean? Who said it? What did they say exactly? He doesn't respond. I'm supposed to see him tonight. I don't think he is so worried about me he would make it up. But who knows. He's a nice guy.

IV.

I didn't think she would come. I walked into the bar with my mountain friend, and another friend from back in the day waved us over. Shit faced and stupid smiles. "Come on come on we are here we see you yes yes," he is saying with his red face and he hugs us both and I am a bit nervous, not because I think she is there but because of the other people I know are there. People I haven't seen. People who will judge me. I don't know, it's not that. I just get nervous when I haven't seen people for a while. I mean, shit. It's been ten years. Anyway. I move over to the table where they all are. I know there are two girls there, I can see them out of the corner of my eye, but I don't look. I hug someone. I don't know who it is. And then she stands up and I know it's her before I look. I look.

She is the most beautiful creature I have ever seen. Still.

I am so sick with nerves and fear I know I am shaking and I say her name like I am surprised and I guess I am but I am lying to her when I say her name like that. Like some stupid question, "you? Oh. You are here? Oh." When I really want to say her name like a man reads a poem or claims a land or titles a sea or honors a God.

Where there is nothing else. Just her name. Where it is the word that tells her - I have been here all along. Waiting for this moment.

We hug and she touches my face and says, "you're hairy," and she is smiling at me. I am so fucking sick I can't talk to her. "Yeah." And I go to hug someone else but brush her side with my hand as I go and say, "you look good," and those words were a little more real. A little closer to how I feel. And I hug someone else and someone else and someone else and then I am in conversation with someone and I am just fucking sick. I don't care what this person is saying to me, "oh you're going to Thailand blahblahblahblah." And it lasts some time before I move on and someone else is "blahblahblahblah"

After a time I go sit down with her and some other girl who is there with a friend of mine and I talk to her but it so choppy and strange. I don't know what we are talking about but I say, "my ex-wife," and she says, "oh you guys broke up?" I say, "yeah". She says, "oh was it mutual or…" and I say, "No. She left me," and then I go talk to someone else and I am thinking *fuck you man what are you doing to me?* She left me… fuck. It's the truth. And I haven't told the truth to a girl I was interested in. It makes me look weak, like shit. I tell them all it was mutual, that we needed to, that I am happy now. But no. I just say, "she left me."

I am talking with two girls now and a guy. But the girls I am doing really well with and we are kind of flirting, you know, nothing serious but of course she comes over. And she stands next to me and looks at my shoes and I can tell she is a little tipsy but not bad. And we start to talk again. And then we both end up standing at the bar and she orders two cups of hot water because she is studying Chinese medicine now. So we are drinking these cups of hot water at the bar and I ask her about her man. "He left me." And I realize this world is a circle.

My mountain friend can see I want her and thinks I am close but he can't help it he needs to go home and I am his ride. So I tell her I need to take him home and say, "come with me," and she says, "okay." So I drive him home and on the way back to the bar I start getting real. I tell her I have thought about her a lot, "probably too much," I say. I tell her she made a real impact on my life and I have never really been able to let her go. I ask to kiss her. She doesn't say no. It's more like, "not right now," or maybe, "not yet." So I tell her I'd like to stay in touch. And she asks when I leave for Thailand, and I say "soon." And I drop her at her car and I go back to my parents' house and just lie in bed looking at the ceiling.

41

Santa Barbara, California is a seasonless place with an almost omnipresent sun that is never too hot. It has money that rolls down the hills of Montecito and comes in on cruise ships from the harbor. You can walk a couple miles from the ocean up State Street all the way to Whole Foods and see everything you need to know about the people that live and visit and shop and work, and the people that sit on the benches with their dogs, flying signs outside of Chipotle asking for a burrito or outside of Starbucks asking for a coffee or outside of some clothing store that sells shirts for hundreds of dollars asking for nickels. And if you veer off State Street to the left and head toward the Mesa you will see small two- and three-bedroom houses on tiny plots of land with cute, simple fences, an orange tree or a palm growing in the front yard. You will see first- and second-generation Mexicans with large families and barbecues on Saturdays and sweet, brown children that play on the sidewalks and you will see college kids that sit on their porches and smoke cigarettes or drink beer in the afternoon. You will also see people trying to live the dream or their version of it, that moved from Wisconsin and Minnesota and Utah and Idaho because they wanted to learn to surf and they wanted the sun and they wanted the sand and they wanted the weather that never changes and they now work two and a half jobs to pay rent and wonder if they should move back home. Nestled at the base of the Mesa before it rises up and drops again into the ocean, there is a two-bedroom house with a little studio apartment that used to be the main bedroom. A sweet, young hippy couple moved from Delaware with their dreams and bought it in the seventies. And they raised three children there for a while until the city felt like it was getting too busy and they moved to Santa Ynez instead and just kept the house.

That is where I lived until I was three and lived again when I was twenty nine. You visited me there once. Maybe twice. It all kind of blends together like so many memories there because the seasons don't exist and because the weather is always the same. The memory that is strongest is the feeling of spaciousness and the way that studio opened up to the sky when I left the doors open and sat on the step below the octopus tree and the bamboo and tried to remember when I was three and felt the efforts of my father all around me in the brick patio and the white walls and the wooden fence with the door that kept my little six by ten brick patio private and allowed me to, when it was dark and scary inside, pull a mat and blanket outside and just look up at the stars and the way the octopus tree let dangle his bulbous leaves twenty feet up in the sky.

I knew I wouldn't live there long. That it is was a transition space for me. I knew I didn't want to be in Santa Barbara and that the people there were not my people, as best as I tried. But I found the things I needed. I would sit on the floor and, later, in that yellow chair and write or I would drive to the nude beach and swim, naked and vulnerable, or I would ride my bike to the rock gym or I would do a job or help my father or draw some art or cry or drive to Santa Ynez for dinner and feel the way my mother worried about me. I'd go up the Mountain and see my friend and the way he worried about me or lay down with a woman in my bed on the floor in the open closet with no doors and make love with her and wonder if my life would ever be truly satisfying or full or whole or if I would be floundering forever and I would feel worried. And I thought about Massachusetts and how we moved there together when we were seventeen and you went to school and I cut lettuce on a farm in Sheffield and money and shelter and food and clothing did not matter because we had each other. I thought about Massachusetts and the way the seasons were separate entities with different colors and different dances and I could tell you that it was summer when our dog went missing and that it was fall when your stepfather died and that it was winter when I waited for you on the Cape and that it was spring when you said you couldn't be with me anymore.

42

Sometimes I think I made it all up. Sometimes I think she never loved me. It was all one-sided. But there are things I remember, things I know happened, things I know she said and things I know she wrote that can't be a different color. Once, in the beginning, when I was in Thailand she wrote:

You are not the guy I meet at a bar and have frivolous sex with to help me get over my last relationship. You are the guy that I camp out with at the beach and look at the stars with and make dinner with and watch movies with and take walks with and stay up all night with.

A month or two later we did most of these things together. Except the camping. That I did on my own but I retraced a trail she told me about and had hiked and camped on with her previous partner years before. I did this because I needed to go backpacking by myself and I wasn't sure where to go. And I did this because I wanted to be closer to her. And when I was out there, alone but with the fear of the sea swallowing me, I felt her as a ghost in the mist that hovered over the sand and made my face wet and salty. I saw her tracks in the sand and smelled her breath in the air. I also felt my need for another body and when the trail opened itself up high above the sea, I felt I could lose myself in the reality of our human solitude and the sun looked at me and I looked back. I know you have felt this way. I know you have seen it lit up and bright and clear and sad and solid. I think we have talked about it, in so many words. But I know we have not talked much about her and how she cast that painful light for me and this is strange because I could have really used a friend to talk about it with. And it makes sense because she was always a bit of a thorn in the side, wasn't she.

I do believe she loved me. She told me this many times.

She also told me she didn't want to be with me.

43

He got out of the car and paid the driver with a fifty baht note and could feel the man's fox eyes follow him across the street as he entered the Soi like he had been there before. As soon as he stepped up the curb, the neon lights entered his bloodstream with a heartbeat and he could taste blood in the air or something like it. A sea of bodies littered the small street swirling around one another. Drunk white men, yelling, red faced in delight and craving, half lit in neon and half cast in shadow, weaved in and out and over one another like a swarm of wasps or wolves or stray children. A Thai man with no legs and one arm and a broken face dragged himself along the street with a cup and looked up at him with both dignity and desperation somehow avoiding, without moving, the constant stomping of unaware feet all around him. A full pig lay longways, speared through ass to mouth and spinning gently over a bed of amber coals. An old Thai woman would occasionally carve a section of the body into plastic bags and place the grisled bits on the front of the cart. Next to her a man sold homemade whiskey and thin Thai men and fat European men stood at the narrow table and took the shots he poured from a bamboo ladle and smiled at one another like old friends. And girls... girls were everywhere. Some were dancing, some serving drinks, some sitting on laps, all with high heels and short skirts and belly shirts or bralettes. All brown and rosy cheeked with black hair that shined red and purple in the neon.

He walked up the Soi until it ended and was surprised to find it was actually quite short and that looking down the other roads from left and right you wouldn't know anything was happening here. Some people walked in the shadows of the street. A couple massage parlors were gently lit. But otherwise the roads were empty and silent.

He turned around and started walking back slower, looking around, and then he saw her. She was short and just a little softer than most of the other girls, their lean Thai bodies like beautiful, brown bamboo, swaying in awkward rhythm around oddly placed poles outside the entrance to every bar. She was talking to someone and smiling and she looked sweet and happy and inviting and open. He walked right up to her then and whoever she was talking to disappeared into the hive of wasps behind him and he could see she was surprised but still open and still smiling and still inviting. She had lipstick on that was pink and brushed pink on her cheeks, a white short-sleeved button-up shirt tied off just below her small breasts, a skirt and high heels, and for a moment they just stood there looking at one another, maybe both equally surprised and equally happy and equally inviting. She reached up and touched his beard and said, "oh so big," and laughed but it was the most gentle laugh he had heard and he laughed and they went inside the bar.

At the bar he bought her a drink. She ordered a Thai whiskey and coke and he got a whiskey and beer and they sat at a little table in the small go-go bar where three girls were dancing on a stage for one customer who wasn't watching and outside Soi Cowboy buzzed in neon and noise. She looked at him and said, "Happy New Year."

"Happy New Year. How do you say it in Thai?"

And she told him and they had another drink. And she told him because it was New Years it was more expensive. "One hundred dollars for the night and you have to pay a tip to the bar."

"All night though, right?"

"Yeah. If you want. All night. No problem."

"Yeah. Okay."

He paid for their drinks and a thirty dollar bar fee to the heavy, middle-aged woman behind the bar as a thin man with dyed hair leaned back against the inside of the bar and watched the transaction. When it was finished the man looked up at him and smiled and nodded. During this transaction she left. She told him she needed to get ready and she went to the back of the bar and slipped up some stairs behind the go-go stage. The woman gave him another beer to sip on and in fifteen minutes she was back, freshly showered with just the lipstick, no blush, no high heels, and a thick, light pink jacket with a small purse that dangled over her arm and looked large on her short body. Her round, young face was warm and confident.

"Sawahdi bi mi," he said to the heavyset woman and the man with the dyed hair and he put his hands together and bowed reverently with a fiery smile. They both broke out in grins and bowed and said, "oh you know Thai language, very good. Very good."

And he left with her.

Outside on the street she took his hand and led him to the little cart with the homemade whiskey and she spoke to the boy with the ladle in Thai and took out some money. She bought a shot for herself and one for him and they drank and then went to the curb. A driver waited there and she spoke to him in Thai and told him the address he had given her. The driver said a price she didn't like and she said, "no, no," and ignored his other offers. She took his hand and pulled him across the street and found an older man smoking outside his car and spoke to him in Thai. He said a price and she liked it. She took his hand and they crawled into the back of the car.

The driver spoke to her in Thai and they had a conversation and at some point they were laughing and smiling and bowing and she turned to him and told him in English that the old man was from the same area of farmland in the north that she was from, just a couple towns away. The driver made eyes at him and smiled and bowed his head.

"You want a drink? Or food? We could stop at a store." He asked her.

"Yeah." And she told the driver in Thai and they found a store and stopped and went inside and she got seaweed snacks with some sort of dried fish and he got some peanuts and a fifth of Sangsom and a bottle of soda because he knew she would want a mixer and then they were back in the car.

They arrived at the hotel and parked and he paid the man and they exchanged a bow. The doorman swimming in his red suit opened the door and bowed deeply for them both. They walked into the lobby past the clerks who bowed to them. He led her to the elevator, pressed the button, the doors opened and they went up to his room on the seventh floor.

The first thing she did when she got inside his room was take off her jacket which she folded neatly on a chair near the window. She then found some of his clothes that he had left in bits and pieces here and there and she took them up on the bed, folded them, opened the deep drawers of a cabinet beneath a large TV and placed them gently inside. She then took his shoes and her sandals, opened the door and put them just outside. Then she made the bed even though it was already made. She pulled the corners of the bedspread tight and tucked it under the pillows. Throughout all of this, he sat in a chair sipping on a glass of whiskey and watched her with utter amusement and admiration and affection. And he was shocked at how bizarre and how normal it all felt. Here she was. Just cleaning up as if they had lived together for years and this was just something she did. There was not a trace of indecency or shame or shadiness.

After she finished she sat on the bed and he poured her a drink and they drank and they talked and although her English was not perfect, it was impressive and it was easy to have a real conversation with her. After a while he kissed her and they made love and her little body wrapped around his and she kissed his ear when he came. Then they showered together and he touched her soft belly in the hot water and loved how she felt and she smiled and her eyes were big and brown and sweet.

They ordered food from the front desk. He called and then she took the phone and spoke Thai and made sure his meal had no meat. "Jai," she said. "Jai ka? Ka ka." And then they were eating together and she turned the TV on and laughed with her mouth full and when they finished she took the plates and put them outside the door.

That night they slept naked together and he took her in his arms and pulled her little, soft body tightly to his own and she just fit there and fell asleep and made cute noises, her thick black hair weaving itself through the tight curls of his beard.

In the morning they kissed and he told her he would see her again soon. And he did, about a month later after he shaved his beard off and they went out to eat and she spoke Thai to the waiter and made sure his food had no meat, "jai. Jai ka? Ka." And she told him about where she grew up and that she had made a choice between being a farmer or coming to Bangkok and dancing go-go and that she was happy she came to Bangkok. She was saving money to open a shop back home. Her parents didn't know what she did for a living but she sent them money here and there and went home often. She was relaxed and open and went home with him that night and they repeated the evening they had a month before but with a lot less whiskey.

44.

.

(letter to you)

Man there is just too much to write about I think. Honestly my first few days in Bangkok were just pretty crazy. And also not that crazy at all. It is really weird. Being here is like a dream I had or am having. Everything seems familiar. It's like - I have definitely lived this already. I am feeling a bit out of touch with the situation I guess. I think not having someone around to share the experience with is extremely odd for me. It would be odd for most people but for me in particular because every big thing I have done for so many years, I did with someone else. I don't know. It is good, just weird.

Today I went to a beach on a teeny tiny boat. The beach was sweet as hell but there are just WAY too many tourists down here. But holy shit it is beautiful here. Huge cliffs and crags. Oh and lots of monkeys! One tried to take my mangoes! It was actually a little scary but I just reacted like he was one of those dudes in Amherst who was hitting on you when we would go out together. I just got all up in this monkey's face and he was like, "whoa, this guy means business." There are also dogs and cats everywhere and everyone is really nice to them. Anyway... still feeling pretty weird.

I am here for some reason.
I just don't know what it is.

-c

45

In Vietnam, in Singapore, on the border of Thailand and Malaysia, in Hat Yai, in Bangkok and in the south of Thailand on the islands and beaches, I found myself wandering from hostel to hostel, dorm to dorm, room to room without direction, surprised that loneliness had not subsided but seemed to hold my hand everywhere I went. I didn't think about you much. Not directly. But you were always there. Pumping through my veins, my body slowly digesting, processing, and attempting to shed you or to remove you or at least remove the person and feelings attached to that person that was no longer part of my reality.

One night at a hostel I was in bed in a dorm room and a couple men were in there, my age, and they asked if I wanted to go out for a drink and I rubbed my long dark beard and said no because I didn't want a drink and because loneliness was weighing so heavily I couldn't move even to accept a gesture of friendship, let alone have a conversation with these guys.

But after sitting in my bunk for another hour doing nothing on the computer, I decided I had to go out. I left the hostel and came onto the open night street and could see the beach and endless flat water of the Gulf of Thailand, a part of the Pacific that somehow connected and crashed onto the shores of California. The smell was like any other beach but the humid air that carried it was different and a breeze was cutting through the humidity like a fan with an ice bucket behind it and I breathed in for a moment and felt that thing called hope.

I went walking and found some stairs leading up to a bar with bright lights blasting out from open walls on the second floor, framed in a bamboo banister and woven roof. I went up. I sat at a table and drank soda water with lime. The place was mostly empty.

A girl came up the stairs and looked around in a shy, sort of curious way. She made her way to the bar in a manner that said she didn't really want a drink but ordered one anyway and she was looking around for something to do and someone to talk to so I reached my hand up and said, "hey. Come sit with me if you want."

She was sipping from two of those tiny little straws that are not made for sipping but for stirring and she raised her eyebrows at me and came and sat down.

"Hey." She said it like she was exhaling.

And we talked about nothing for another drink or two and then I asked her if she wanted to take a walk with me and she said she did.

Out from the bar, down the stairs, away from the lights and down the sidewalk that lined the beach where no cars were driving. We walked. It was moon-lit and shining from the sky and from the water and the breeze had warmed but the air had cooled. No mosquitos. The sound of water rippling against sand. Palm trees and the smell of brine. We walked and we talked about nothing.

Then I took her hand. And she recoiled as if I had punched her. And I can't remember what she said. "I have a boyfriend," or maybe, "I'm not looking for that." But I do remember feeling confused and also, that it was funny. Not that she was upset by my gesture of connection, but that I was so lonely and that from the deepest pit of my soul I had collected myself from a sunken bed in a dorm with a computer on my lap, to wade through the thick night air to a bar where I reached out to this girl who said, "yes," and then said, "no" - and that somehow this was a circle, a cycle, a pattern. That this was my rock to push up and lose and collect and push up again.

But of course, I wonder what more is here. What her story would be if asked about that night when the man with the beard and blood in his shoes took her hand and looked at her with such sad eyes. *What happened inside of you? What did you see in his face? What did you smell in the air? Was the moon out or was it dark? Was the air cool and the wind warm or was it the other way around?*

We walked back to the bar and kept talking about nothing.

I went back to the dorm soon after. It was empty for another few hours. I lay in bed and smiled at myself and the ridiculousness of the rock I was pushing and thought,

what the fuck am I doing here?

In the morning I woke up early and caught a long boat to an island. I sat in the hollowed-out boat with its skinny motor screaming behind me and my beard opening up against my face from the wind and a tall brunette by my side. She was with her friend. She had a boyfriend, she said. She wasn't sure they were going to stay together. I told her I was recently divorced. We weren't yet. Not technically. But it was easier than describing what "separated" meant. I talked too much about it or I looked too sad or she saw something or smelled something in the air. She left the boat without acknowledging me much. Later that day I sat on a crowded beach and saw her pass with her friend. She looked up and saw me and turned her head and said something to her friend and they both kept their gaze forward and kept moving.

I went for a walk. I bought some mangoes. Some aggressive monkeys tried to take them right out of my hands. They yelled at me and glared their teeth. Without thinking I stomped my foot in front of them and yelled back and they hesitated, then danced away.

I sat on a rock off the trail. I wandered back to the beach. I got in the water. I looked at my hands. "Here I am," I tried to tell myself, but it didn't work. I got out of the water and went to find a place to stay. I wandered around the small village built just for tourists and didn't like it. I caught a long boat back to the mainland. I got a private room at the hostel I had stayed at the previous night and alone, I slept.

In the morning I got on a bus and after a long day on the road where I saw, not one, but two busses just like the one I was in, crashed, one into an electric pole and the other turned over in the middle of the highway, I was dropped off in Hat Yia where I eventually found a barber shop, sat down in a chair and told the Thai man and his wife to cut my beard. They spoke no English but after twenty minutes I paid fifty Baht and left with my darkness on the floor and my skin, white, naked and frightened.

46.

(talks with men)

"Hey"

"Sup dude."

"I've got a date for you."

"Oh yeah, how's that?"

"One of the sisters."

"Which one."

"The one with the kid."

"The little one or the big one?

"Little."

"I like that one."

"I know you do."

"What do you mean you got a date for me?"

"Wedding. You got a suit?"

"Haha. I got a suit bro. The one you saw me get married in."

"It's a nice suit."

"Damn straight."

47

He had his friend tie his tie just like he had done on his wedding night except this time it was in Santa Barbara instead of in some country town in Connecticut on the border of Massachusetts. They left the house and drove to the courthouse. They watched the wedding on stiff, wooden benches, a mural on the walls of men on horses and saints with crosses and boats and rocks and the sea spilling out form the plaster and nearly coming to life on the Mediterranean tile floor. The ceremony was soft and quick and left no lasting memory but he can still see the eyes of the horses on the walls that followed them as they left the courthouse. Then everyone was walking out the doors and through the sunken garden and down the street to an old mission where tables and music and a build-your-own taco bar merged together on the open dirt courtyard. The sun was still high but it was becoming evening and the ocean exhaled from over the mountain and her breath was cool and came to rest over the mission roof and pushed some dirt around the chairs.

He got some veggies fried in too much oil and a couple tortillas and sat at one of the tables. She was sitting next to him. She was wearing a simple dress with flowers and a sort of shawl over her shoulders. Her brown hair laid like summer straw down her back and reminded him of pictures he had seen of his mother when she was young and wore Levis and went camping out of an old bus in the redwoods with his father who had a thick black beard.

Next to her was her sister, taller and much more talkative and beside her, her sister's date who was, somehow, already drunk and boisterous and then his mountain friend, with nearly two decades of memories between them, and his friend's girlfriend. She was sweet and freckled and quiet and somewhat broken and when he had seen her naked at the nude beach, she had held her head down against the sun and touched her belly tenderly when no one was looking and maybe it was because she was freckled and quiet or maybe because she was somewhat broken, but he felt a special sort of tenderness towards her and sometimes wanted to protect her from the world.

They all ate and the music played and most of them drank a few drinks until the sun was exhausted and quickly sank behind the hills and into the ocean casting a bright eye on the San Rafael mountains, turning them auburn, ruddy and wood yellow. She had a couple drinks and she was warm and he could see it on her cheeks.

"You want to dance?"

He took her hand. They walked into the open patch of dirt and sand where a string of lights cast little glowing circles onto the adobe walls behind the DJ. He took her and pulled her close to his body and they moved together. Some other couples were dancing but they knew each other and they were bored with themselves. But this, between them, was new and fresh and she was warm and he could see it on her face and he was calm and strong and held her easily and without thought and when the music slowed he only pulled her closer. He pushed his nose into her neck and smelled her and kissed her collarbone and she pulled him close to her and her hair wrapped itself around his face like a meadow and her breath smelled like spring.

48

It was early morning. The sun was cresting through trees, lifting a light fog steaming from the streets and leaves. He was driving in the big Chevy Cummins from Florence to Westhampton to plant some trees, to move some mulch, to build a wall, to run a lawn mower. He was feeling clear and listening to music on his headphones as the truck swayed like a whale over the smooth hills of Route 10 and then onto Route 66.

He was thinking of his high school girlfriend and the conversation he'd had the night before with his friend about her.

"She died."

"No way..."

"Yeah man."

"Fuck... what happened?"

"Well, here's the thing, the details are super sketchy because she was in Dubai. She lived there. She's a flight attendant there. Was. I guess... She was found in her room. She was strangled to death. They think the husband did it. But it's really hard to find any info, just one super short article."

"...Fuck me. Strangled.... I was just thinking about her..."

And then he had gone to sleep and woken up and he had loved the world for no reason at all. And he thought about her as he drove - her, back then, when she'd written him a note in Japanese that he'd kept for years and never knew what it said. And one night when they'd been naked together and she'd looked into his eyes and said, "there is so much here." And she was that other girl who'd taken him by the hand and led him across the street and laid him down in those pea fields and kissed him deeply, one day before flying back home to Japan for the summer.

He slowed and turned into the narrow dirt drive, the sweating mulch piles breathing into the morning as he drove past and the small potted shrubs, trees, and bushes stood erect and still and waiting. He parked outside of the big garage and he took his headphones out of his ears and turned off the truck and the whale fell asleep, all movement stopped and the silence of the morning came in from the windows. He sat there for a while - the first one to arrive - and just stared at the back of the green house. Eventually he got out of the truck, went into the big garage, grabbed a broom and started sweeping the fermenting grass clumps left by the mowers on the concrete floor, pushing them out onto the dirt and thinking about her deep brown, black eyes and wishing he still had that note.

49

It was the first date I had after you. I met her on a dating site. We met at a cafe in Florence. She got a milkshake. I got a water. I had stopped drinking then and I had started running and I was losing weight and my eyes were clearing up. I was in a new body, in a new world without you, doing something I never thought I would have to do again and I had no idea what I was doing. We took our drinks and walked down the bike path behind the cafe, the one that used to be the railroad and goes all the way to Belchertown in one direction and up to Turners Falls in the other. We walked towards Turners where you cross over the road and next to the river where you can take a little path out to the top of a waterfall and jump in. We just kept to the path and talked about who knows what as she sipped her milkshake and we both were sweating. She reminded me of my sister in the way that she felt all set, independent and needing nothing, and in height, shorter than me. I think she wore her sunglasses the whole time. Her face was cute like one of those little Troll Dolls, but not unattractive at all. I know I didn't know how to touch her, let alone kiss her, let alone share anything real and when she asked about something I talked about you and tried to convince us both that it was all in the past but neither of us believed that and we walked back to the cafe and hugged and I walked home.

We met again a few days later. It was the Fourth of July and she was at that park on the border of Northampton and Florence in between Route 9 heading north and Route 9 heading south. I drove my truck there. We talked a little. She told me she was in a roller derby club and seemed very serious about it - but she laughed at me when I told her I was in a bicycle gang where we would all get together and just ride our bikes around at night. We had jackets with patches that symbolized our initiation into the Pythons and our bandanas were purple. Just a bunch of misfits in our late twenties who somehow came together and shared friendship for a few short months. I had found them with my friend through a post on Craigslist. We went to their first meet-up because we were both sad and lonely and life was feeling confusing and directionless and somewhat humorous and dark and we needed something light-hearted and distracting. It made sense she laughed but it also hurt and my shoes felt soggy.

She was leaning against a tree and I don't remember how it happened but I got close to her or maybe it was when we were hugging goodbye and I faced her face and we kissed. I remember the way her tongue snaked into my mouth and slithered over my own. I remember her saliva. And I remember that moment when she exhaled a little bit, her mouth open on mine and I breathed in and some fireworks went off behind us somewhere in the park. It was dark out and she left and I walked back to my truck. I felt electricity running through me and when I pulled out of my spot I ran over a bit of the curb and I forgot to turn my lights on for a second and then saw the cop car behind me and I turned them on. I made a left onto 9 heading north back to Florence and he pulled me over. Soon another car was there and then another and then there were three of them, three cars and three cops, all out of their cars and all shining their lights on me.

"You lighting those fireworks?"

"No. I was just walking with this girl."

"You have fireworks in here?"

"No. I was just meeting up with this girl and we were walking."

"You know it's illegal to light off fireworks in Massachusetts. Where are they?"

"I don't have any."

"Why did you try to boogie out from the park like that? Huh?"

"I don't have fireworks. Man, I don't care about fireworks. I kissed this girl just now. We were meeting up to walk around and we kissed. It's the first girl I kissed since my ex-wife, okay? I don't have any fireworks."

"Okay. I'm happy you kissed a girl but we got people lighting off fireworks over there and then you pull out and boogie down the road, what am I supposed to think?"

And they shined their lights around the cab and looked through some trash I had in bags in the bed and then told me I could go. I left and nothing had changed. I laughed and the electricity ran through my body and some fireworks went off behind me as I drove back home.

I didn't see her again after that. I went on some other dates. I moved into my garage in Belchertown. I quit my job and went back to school for a semester to finish my degree. I let my beard grow big and black and dark. I continued not to drink and I kept running and started swimming, too, and lost more weight and my eyes got a little clearer and I went on more dates and they became less awkward and I met a girl in NYC and I told her I loved her and I did for a month until I didn't and it was sad but it was okay. I kept meeting up with the bike gang because I was still mourning and lonely and felt directionless and needed something to laugh about until I went on a date with a small girl from Turkey in big black boots, eyeliner, and dyed red hair who walked a mile to meet up with me at the park in Northampton and something stuck and she became my first girlfriend after you. And when she washed her face before we had sex for the first time and I saw her without makeup, I fell in love. I stopped meeting up with the bike gang and instead, she and I spent our time building mountains.

50

Up on the mountain he went to her house and the other sister, the fiesty one, was there with her friend and everyone was fiery after wedding dances and drinks. Fiery, under the shelter of a small light powered by DC; fiery, free from the car and the darkness, driving up those curves for nearly an hour where the shale loomed, ready to pounce. And eventually the other sister took the friend and they were left there and before anything unfolded she said, "yes, you can spend the night." And soon they were kissing at the kitchen table and then went upstairs to the little cove of a room with a mattress on the floor and gentle lace covering a squat glass window that looked out into the arms of an oak tree. He stripped the flowers from her body and dropped the dress onto the floor. They made love and then made love again and he liked the way she kissed and the way her breasts were, soft and a little low. And later, she told him she hadn't made love to anyone in a long time. "What's long?" he asked and she said a couple of years. And they went to sleep together and he took her body and pulled it into his and it just fit there. The next morning he met her son. The small boy was smart and angry that a strange man was in his house and that made sense and he left them and got a ride down the mountain in his suit with his jacket and tie tucked to his side.

A couple days later they met for Indian food. She insisted he order for her and so he did and when the food came she stood up from the table and took one of the empty plates and put food on it. Curry and vegetables and rice and naan and placed it down in front of him. Then she sat back down and made another plate for herself. And she waited to take a bite of her food until he did. And he thought of the Thai girl in his hotel in Bangkok folding his clothes and placing his shoes outside of the door and although it was strange to be served in such a way, it was also nourishing and sweet and he felt his lungs take in a little more air.

They went to his small studio apartment and she taught him some keys to play on the keyboard and they sang together and she stood behind him at one point, as he sat in the small yellow chair and pressed on the keyboard and her hands were down his chest and her head lay over his shoulder and she sang a beautiful song. They made love and fell asleep on the thin piece of foam on the floor and she lay on his shoulder all night and made small noises when the dreams overtook her and twitched like a rabbit.

A few days after that they were together at a market eating some fruit and she told him about the Apocalypse and Jesus and being saved and all so casually there was nothing really to say. He just felt very clearly that he would stop seeing her. But in that moment he just took it in and listened to the waves down the mesa crashing onto the shore.

51

Chiang Mai is a comforting and easy place. It is also sometimes loud and difficult not to feel the pulse of the concentrated energy that resonates from inside the old city walls and slips over the surrounding moat and through the gates that open to new apartments, condos, hotels and old bungalows. To patches of farmland and infinite temples with golden peaks calling up to God and God radiating back through every sun that rises over the mountains and every sun that sets just beyond Doi Suthep. Thai and foreigner integrate and move together here, in a gentle dance of give and take and smile and bow and hello and sawadi kap. Massage, food, hostel, laundry, coffee, papaya salad, vendors sitting on the ground, coconuts, scooters, exhaust, baht, alleys, sois, streets, traffic, malls, brown skin, brown eyes, brown lips, all floating through the city participating in one giant play that you can't help but feel a part of. It is an epic act of color and smell and sound that repeats itself, with very little change, every day, where rice is cooked and bagged and sold for pennies and oranges are pressed, bottled and put on ice and 7-Eleven never ends, just changes its workers, all some variation of small, brown, sweet, and awkward. Men push carts full of useless items and women cut pineapple or through the sinews of chickens and children go to school in uniforms and monks accept meals for the day that include chocolate bars or bags of chips at four in the morning, shoeless and orange-robed. Here, God's hand rests itself gently over all movement and action and thought and it is so difficult to find anger or urgency, and loneliness feels softer because everywhere there are bows and smiles.

I've always envisioned you here on vacation, slowing down enough to really see it the way I have seen it. You might love it if you let yourself.

I think it could even change your life.

After traveling around Southeast Asia for a month by myself, aloof and lost and often depressed and always lonely, I went to Chiang Mai and, there, I created a bond with a handful of other men. They were all younger, all focused on healing in one way or another and all a bit aloof and lost and often depressed. . But we all moved into the same building. We went to the markets together, we lay in the park together, we rode bikes, and we talked about women. We made food and listened to music and danced around and hugged each other and during those weeks we were, none of us, alone. But I'm pretty sure, in our own ways, we were all a bit lonely. And I thought a lot about you and I thought a lot about her and longed for a past with you while fantasizing a future with her. And even though at the time I was, in many ways, the most present I had been in a decade, I was living in a world of memories and in a world of dreams.

We met up at that park down the hill from the mission where you have to drive next to the rock wall on that skinny road with the ravine on the other side and constantly look out for bicyclists in their mid-forties with pouch bellies and greying hair, gratifying themselves by grazing death's hands as they whip around blind curves and curse the cars that don't see them fast enough. That park. I turned off the road and over the little dry creek and found her sitting on top of a table, her feet on the bench and her long body curled into itself as she leaned her weight onto her knees with her elbows, one hand cradling her wide German jaw as she watched her dark son play with sticks and stones.

She saw me walking toward her and she put her feet down on the ground and stood up like a crane landing in water, long and awkward and beautiful. She was tall and stronger than how she held her shoulders beneath that oversized sweater. Her son stopped all movement and holding a stick in one hand, stared at me. She smiled and moved toward me on long legs and we hugged and maybe she bent down a little so I didn't get too buried in her collarbones. She was beautiful and grand and held herself in a way that denied both and it was the same when we were in high school and I watched her walk across the courtyard between classes, lean and white with long, straight hair flowing behind her slightly collapsed spine that softened her height protected her in some way and for some reason I could only guess. She was a grade above me in high school and I thought she was beautiful and independent and cool and I think we spoke only a few words back then.

"Hi."

"Hi. Wow what a trip. You look really good."

"Yeah. You too. It's been so long."

"Over ten years I think."

"This is my son."

"Hey dude."

The boy stood looking at me with that stick in his hand, coyote eyes, frozen and then he wasn't - he smiled with a missing tooth and said, "look," and held up the stick at me.

We stayed there for an hour maybe. Talking and watching her son move things around and she said she was going to go to her parents' house and I should come if I wanted. I could stay there, they had lots of rooms and it was a long drive.

Why not.

So I drove for about an hour north up 101 but instead of turning right to head to Buellton and back to the Santa Ynez Valley like I normally would, I turned left on the slow road towards Lompoc and, nestled in those low rolling hills was a dusty drive to a little farm house. She came out to greet me and we went inside and sat at a stubby, wooden table and I met her brother who offered me a drink but I said no thank you. Her son was there and he needed attention but no one knew how to give it to him so the space was uncomfortable and I felt something then from her and from her brother and from the burden of legacy and how they gently but overtly denied that young child something and it kept me from fantasizing about a life with her I felt his restlessness when he squirmed and cried and went to his room and she sort of shrugged it off with a smile. It wasn't evil. It just reminded me of something and it sat inside of me when I would see her and I think it kept my heart a little closed, you know? I felt the force in it and the way her traumas and her burdens were being laid upon him. And there was this moment I felt like I was the boy and you were his mother and I wondered - Did I cry like that? Did you shrug me off? Was I dark? Did I ask you to be my mother? Did you ask me? Or does it all go back further than that, further than you?

We smoked some pot. I wasn't really smoking then so I must have just had a little and I'm sure I was pretty stoned. I think we played a board game. I liked her brother. He was a bit drunk and didn't seem to treat me as a threat. He was blond and thick. When it was time to sleep she led me outside and dropped me off at some other, smaller cottage a ways from the house. I lay down and thought how funny it was that I came out here and that I liked it. How funny it was that I had only recently friended her on Facebook and maybe the day before we exchanged a message. It was all funny and I liked myself for doing it. And I liked her. But I fell asleep thinking about that dark child and that stick and those coyote eyes.

54

Hat Yai is dirty and heavy and dense and a little rough or cruel or displeased with the world. Old women sit in plastic chairs on tiled floors in empty storefronts below four-story buildings and quietly glare at you while you pass. Greasy ducks hang by their necks and shimmer behind glass, yellow and orange in restaurant lighting and vats of boiling broth steam into the already humid air. Rice is served, scooped from a bowl and formed on a plate. There are two types of beer in tall bottles that don't come cold but are served with a glass of ice and you might wonder about the source of the frozen water. Small bars open early and stay open late, playing difficult-to-digest pop music that spills like a bucket of dirty water onto the sidewalk and rough road. Dark Thai men with religious caps smoke in doorways and talk in harsh tongues. Massage parlors are pink and smell like baby oil and cheap perfume. Foreigners are Malaysians up from the border to drink all night or Chinese, arguing over the price of a room with the old women in plastic chairs in empty storefronts. There is nothing to see in Hat Yai. You just walk around and wonder if you should leave today or tomorrow.

55.

(letters to you)

I.

I'm alive. Can't get my other account to open or find a plug for comp so my battery is going to die like now. Just wanted to tell you I love you before that happens. I will be in touch tomorrow when I get to Bangkok.

- c

II.

Got to Bangkok. So Taipei was a lot of fun. I got a ride to downtown for about thirty bucks and then walked around with my big backpack on for about eight hours or so and saw some old guys in this big park doing strange exercises and attractive girls that laughed at my beard and a billboard of Brad Pitt. Very clean city. At least the part I was in. With a lot of boring people. After that trek I went back to the airport and just passed out all over the place until the plane for Bangkok left where I slept the entire way. When I got to the hotel it was about two thirty AM and I saw a bunch of white dudes with Thai girls coming back wasted. This morning... no. This evening, about five PM or so I heard the slap slap slap of thigh to ass and a Thai girl moaning the strangest sounds. It didn't last long but it was crystal clear. Not much insulation between these walls.

Everyone is ridiculously nice. Thai women are very pretty. I don't know what they think of my beard but I am the only one around that I have seen, including whites, with a beard of any kind. Or a piercing in my face. Not many Thais have piercings or tattoos that I have seen. So far, though, I haven't made it much further than the hotel room so I can't say for certain. I need to go down to the crazy sex market to get a good idea of how weird shit can get around here. I was going to go tonight but the night market for food and other shit is closed and I am pretty hungry.

Today is New Years Eve so I am going to go to downtown Bangkok and check out all the insane drunks. After that I will go South. I don't have any plans yet but Bangkok is very fucking hot and gross and I don't want to stay here much longer. What I have seen of the forests driving in look spectacular and I really want to get into them soon.

So far I haven't met anyone but I haven't tried either. I have just been sleeping sleeping sleeping.

Write me back.

Love

- c

III.

Everything you said in your previous email seems pretty right on. I don't know about any of it anymore. I was really happy with you but I was also really dependent on you. I am not sure that I could have separated myself from us and still kept us. I think I needed to be left because I certainly wouldn't have done it. I wish things hadn't been so rough the last few years for us but it all is just part of what was now. Now I need to be careful. I am really afraid of being caught and falling back into old habits. I was following my old footsteps with that goth girl from Turkey. And even now I question myself. I question breaking things off with her and coming to Thailand, knowing full well that I would have been unhappy staying there and staying with her. I would do it just so I wouldn't have to feel the pain of not having her. Just the same way that I would have done anything to stay with you and to keep us together and that was exactly the problem. Or one of the problems... Anyway, I'm just trying not to get lost in that again.

I'm heading to a place called Hat Yai tomorrow. We'll see if it changes anything.

- c

56

I remember sending you emails the first time I went to Thailand and I shared some stories and I shared some feelings but I kept a lot from you. Perhaps I kept a lot from myself too. I was straddling worlds then and I was, in the in-between, lost and I knew it.

I moved around a lot for a while because I was trying to outrun your shadow or the shadow of our relationship or maybe to catch the light of the relationship I was forming in my mind with that girl from the pea fields. The one you didn't like. The one I kissed when we were married because one day I went to California to pick up the blue Ford Ranger your stepfather built for us and drive it back to Massachusetts and while I was there I went to a music festival at Lake Cachuma and she was there and you were not. I hadn't seen her in about seven or eight years. She shared a beer with me and she dipped her head and looked at me in this way... I kissed her because of that look and because I was still fourteen somewhere inside of myself and wanted redemption and because I didn't know what it all meant.

Yeah. Her.

I was putting it all on her. Our entire relationship and you and the way we loved each other and the things we thought and the words we said and the ideas I had and the colors I saw and the sounds you made. All of it. The whole house we built. I was moving those bricks from our broken building into a bag to drop inside her door when she opened it for me.

But she hadn't opened it yet. So I was just carrying those bricks around Southeast Asia, tired, and pretending nothing was on my back. But with every woman who opened up to me, I think I left one brick at her feet, and in that way, left a little more of my burden behind me. I didn't know that one day I would need to collect them all, especially the bag I did eventually drop in her house, to rebuild what we had built. To look at it. To remember it. To go inside of it and then to walk away and let the earth do what it does. And of course, this is all easy to see in reflection.

At the time, I picked up my bag of bricks, I reached for the light, I ran from the shadow and I moved from the south of Thailand. I took a bus to Hat Yai and I found a room somewhere in the city across the street from a restaurant with ducks in the window. The room was dark and I put my things down and lay on the bed in the early morning. I felt uncomfortable and I rubbed my beard. I left the room and went across the street and ordered a plate of rice and vegetables and thought about buying a beer but didn't. After, I paid and went for a walk trying not to get lost by turning around every so often and taking in the view from the opposite direction.

The city was hollow.

The sun lived and died behind a film of humid cloud. There were few shops and most were closed. There were few people on the sidewalk or the street even though the buildings were three or four stories high and dense with rooms with small windows, some with shutters, some with drapes, but most just a pane of glass and open to the air. I didn't like it. Something felt wrong about this place. Or maybe it was me.

I passed two old women in plastic chairs in an empty storefront and they fell silent and watched me and glared. Around the corner a pink massage sign emerged like the head of the plastic flowers you sometimes see stapled to live stalks of green and it takes you a second to understand why something feels wrong about that plant. Under the sign and on the three steps that led to the door of the massage parlor, four women sat talking but stopped when they saw me and one stood and beckoned me - *come inside* - and they all said in varied pitch, "massage."

I had never had a massage anywhere but in the States and only a handful of times and I wasn't really sure I wanted one but I was carried away by the acknowledgement of my existence and went in and they gave me some clothes to change into and I was led upstairs and lay down on a small bed on the floor and a sheet was pulled around me that hung on a wire and created a little room for me. A young girl, maybe twenty, had me lie on my back and she massaged me gently and firmly and perhaps a little sensually and this went on for maybe fifteen minutes until another woman, a little older, pulled the sheet aside and knelt beside me and said in a hushed and broken English, "you want special massage?"

I didn't understand her.

"Special massage. You want?" she said again.

Okay.

"My friend watches, okay? She my student. She learn. She watches, okay?" And she gestured to the young girl.

Okay.

Then the woman took my pants off and, on her knees, scooted up close to me and draped my legs on either side of hers, spreading me open the way I would spread a woman open and the juxtaposition immediately turned me on and frightened me and I felt small and relaxed and excited and anxious. The younger girl sat on her knees to the side of me and studiously observed. The woman put some oil on her hands and began to rub my thighs and below my balls and over my asshole and then up over my belly and then back down and up again. Slowly, slowly and she waited until I had been erect and swollen for some time before touching my head and shaft. And when she did, her touch was gentle and firm, confident and sensual and she delicately massaged my balls and under my balls and pressed on my asshole and pushed down on my belly and I had - never - felt anything like that. And all the while this young girl just sat next to me watching. After a time she sent the young girl away as she thought it was interfering with me and placed my hands on her thighs as she kept rubbing me. She took off her shirt and pulled her breasts out of her bra and placed my hands on them and kept rubbing me and I came. Then she lay down on my chest and asked if I wanted the young girl to finish the massage or her. I told her she could finish if she wanted. And that's what she did. She put her shirt back on and used a small washcloth to clean me up and then finished massaging my arms and legs and back and shoulders and neck and head. And at the end she showed me her Facebook account and asked me to add her but I didn't have any internet and I sort of just wanted to get away so I told her I would find her later and I wrote down her name on a piece of paper and I left.

I found my way back to the street where I was staying and I went into the restaurant and ordered more rice and vegetables and a tall beer. They brought the beer first with a tall glass of ice and opened it for me at the table and I poured it over the ice and drank and wondered where that frozen water had come from. I ate. I drank some more. I went back to my room and lay down for a bit.

Later I went to a bar. It was a small room with a tall ceiling - cavern-like. The walls were dark and dirty and things were peeling off from the corners and the light was low from twisted, metal sconces that protruded awkwardly at eye level like they were starting a fight but didn't care about seeing it through. The bartender ignored me as long as he could and finally poured me a whiskey and put a large, sweating beer on the counter. The music was loud and irritating. Most of the tables were occupied with men drinking, all sullen, Thai and Chinese. A group of Malaysian men and women danced in a small opening on the chipped, tile floor where spotlights of soft yellow and fuchsia marked the territory for movement. And they moved in unknowing, awkward gyrations and drank and took shots at the bar and yelled when Gangham Style came on.

I watched one of the women move and laugh, her dark hair cut above her shoulders and her breasts bouncing heavily on her small chest in a white shirt. She was smiling and had one dark front tooth. Her skin was yellow brown like the broth boiling in restaurants where noodles are dipped and cooked and I wanted to drink her. I ordered more whiskey at the bar and watched her move and as the night went on people stopped at the bar and were pulled into the energy of that group of awkward dancing Malaysians until the bar was full and a dozen people were dancing in the small square of chipped tile and the cigarette smoke swirled in the colors of the spotlights. I didn't dance but took my beer and walked over to the girl with the dark tooth, her hair falling over her face as she danced and I said hi.

"Hi," she said.

"Where are you from?"

"Malaysia." She said it like Ma-lay-zee-ah.

"I like the way you dance."

"Thank you."

She didn't want to talk to me. I rubbed my beard and thought I must look a little crazy. But I was also a little drunk, so I took the pain of rejection and put it in my pocket for later and asked what she was doing here. She never stopped dancing as she told me she had travelled up from Malaysia with the rest of her insurance company. They had had a good year and her boss was taking them to party in Thailand where things were more "relaxed." And then a man came up to me. A young guy. Chinese. The boss. He was wearing glasses and a jacket and a button up shirt that was hanging loosely on his small body. He stood between the girl and me and put his hands together and bowed as deeply as possible and told me he didn't want any trouble.

"This is my worker. I am responsible for all of these workers." And he bowed again. "No trouble, okay?"

And in that moment, I felt him take me for something I was not. I told him it was no problem and I found an empty table and finished my beer and watched them dance and laugh and I decided I would leave in the morning.

I went back to my small room and fell asleep. In the morning I packed my bags but left them in the room. I went out and down the street and found a barber shop with a Thai man and his wife and they spoke no English but I pulled on my beard and said, "cut," and they did. When I left the air hit my face with startling intimacy and I felt naked and exposed and opened up, spread wide and emptied out. I picked up my bags and left the key in the room and found a car to the train station.

57

He called her.

"Hey. What are you up to?"

"I just put my son to bed. What are you doing?"

"Just wanted to see if you want to come over."

"Yeah. I can do that."

"Your son is okay?"

"Oh yeah. My grandparents are here. I will tell them."

"Alright. See you soon."

And twenty minutes later she knocked on his door and he opened it up and she came in. They drank some tequila that was in his freezer and they made out in his tiny hallway and she slid down the wall to meet his face. Her long legs bent on either side of his and her blond hair wrapped around his neck.

"We're not going to have sex," she said.

"I know," he said. And he meant it.

And then they were having sex on that thin foam roll in the open closet where he slept and he was on top of her. Those long legs pulled up so her knees were next to his cheeks and he looked at her strong jaw and her eyes closed and her lips just slightly open and they breathed heavily and made noises together. Her breath smelled like warm milk and he breathed it in and was nourished.

A few days later they were walking on the bluffs of Carpentaria where you can look down at the squat shore and watch seals come in to sunbathe and to mate. A rookery, they call it. They watched those slick, blue bodies roll around in the waves and turn their bellies up to the sun for a while before getting back into her car where she drove him to an empty farmhouse she used to stay in before the county kicked her out for occupying an illegal dwelling. It sat a half mile off 101 surrounded by citrus in a grove owned by her parents. They parked and went in. The bed was made up and colorful bits of cloth hung from windows and changed the sunlight from yellow to pink and the room was warm. They made love and then went outside naked and took a shower together from a pipe that ran from somewhere up through decking and attached to the outside wall under an eave. She was beautiful. Magnificent really. Strong and soft and long and she didn't say much, just rubbed the cool water around on his chest and pressed her body into his.

And a few days after that they were driving somewhere and he told her he wasn't looking to get too deep in a relationship at the moment. He was processing some things around his ex-wife and this other girl, "you know her actually," he said, and told her who it was and she just nodded and said it was okay and that she understood. It was relieving to set a boundary that was, in fact, not really for her but more for himself. They saw each other a few more times after that, until they didn't.

58.

(poem)

 i met a woman in the woods
she was an archer
i lay down with her in the woods
i lay down with her
and her arrows
and the skin of other animals

59

I landed in California with my beard shaved off and a couple days later I took the train to see her. You can't imagine what it felt like for me. You and I were talking at that point, but it wasn't something I could share with you. You knew I was sort of seeing her or sort of about to start seeing her but you didn't know what it felt like. It was too tender. Too real. Too much. You were six months pregnant then and I didn't want to burden you. And honestly, it was… too important, too young, too fragile to share with you because it became intertwined with my survival. And if I wanted to keep breathing, to keep evolving, to keep moving, to keep shedding you, I needed to keep it safe.

The train left from Lompoc and rolled through the dunes and sea grass. The car was empty and outside it was gray and blue and the sand was light yellow. I thought about her face and the way her lips were full and her freckles were the color of the sun that came through the gray in sudden and unexpected bursts, so bright it forced my eyes closed and I breathed in - This was the change I had been waiting for. In some city, I switched from a train to a bus and in the parking lot I watched a dirty man in three jackets digging in the trash. On the bench just next to him sat a college kid with his hands in his pockets wearing a big set of black headphones over his ears and a bleak and emotionless expression on his face. The only movement I felt was my blood and for a moment I could see everything, still as a picture.

I got on the bus and it bounced around on the road until the sun went down and I sent her a text when I was close. "I'll be there," she texted back. I got out of the bus at the small station in Santa Cruz and I waited under an orange halogen light, like a theater spotlight before the audience arrives. She pulled in twenty minutes later in a Subaru hatchback using the bus entrance and before I was able to open the door, a cop on foot told her she couldn't park there but I was already halfway in and she was playing stupid and smiled and said, "sorry," but of course she knew what she was doing and it was clear she had been drinking but only I noticed. We drove away.

"Hi." She turned and looked at me and her face was red in the dark with drink and things I didn't know about then.

"Hi."

We parked at her place and got out and got inside and I guess it was then that we hugged in her tiny home with the white bed and the fridge and the sofa and a yellow chair she wanted to get rid of and the hot tub outside and the owner's house close by and the flowers growing at the door and the night and all that heavy shit I had brought with me and just put down right there and thought to myself how wrong everyone had been, never really knowing what she was thinking.

Later we made love. I smelled her skin and her armpits and pubic hair and her pussy and her breath. I came inside her and imagined us having children even though I knew she had started taking the pill just so I could come inside her and not have children. And I lay down next to her and panted and pulled her close and we cuddled that way for a time. Then she got up naked and stayed naked and put some needles in my arm, practicing her acupuncture. One needle caught and she pulled it out and put it back in and pulled it out again and put it back in, sort of laughing as she did it. I didn't care. But an hour later I had a reaction or a purge or maybe it wasn't related at all. I just got deathly ill and found myself on her couch shivering and sweating for half the night. I was alone there and she slept in her bed until sometime early in the morning she came to check on me and she stroked my face and I pulled her close to me and we kissed and my body cooled and we made love there on the couch and again played out our roles and again I became a child and again she became a mother.

In the morning I was no longer sick and we went out for bagels and I just got one plain, toasted with tomatoes. Then we went to the beach and on the way I played with her hand as she drove and her long, strong fingers moved around mine like snakes born and she looked at me and had the eyes of a devil and the eyes of sadness and the eyes of fear and the eyes of mystery and these things are so close together we lose ourselves in attempting to name them and it is easier just to say "and she looked at me."

Before I'd gone to Thailand and had come back; took the train to Santa Cruz, and saw her for the first time in seven or eight years, I had thought about making love with her. And I thought, then, I would die if we did. I am certain now, that is, in part, true. Death and birth and burdens were built and crumbled and shuffled around for a very long time after that. I wove myself deeply into her with roots that, to this day, continue to detangle themselves and find the health of being rooted into the earth instead of rooted to an idea of something that never truly existed. I wonder how much you understand this. I wonder what roots you unwove from me and which roots I unwove from you. And which roots we still have tangled together somewhere deep down below the black mud, worms, and bedrock.

60.

(letters to her)

I.

I have been actively keeping myself from writing you. I was trying to go for two weeks. I almost made it. I have thought about you a lot, but I don't want to confuse your life or mix up your healing process. I hope this email doesn't do that. For now, I will keep it short.

I just arrived in Singapore. I have had a good journey so far. A lot of moving. It seems I can't stay in any one place more than forty-eight hours. Right now I think that is okay. Strange thing - this all feels very familiar. Have you had that when traveling? I wonder if it is common.

The sun is setting now over Chinatown, Singapore and from my hotel window I can see the pink and gray of the clouds peeking around the tops of high rises. I am going to go out on the street and see if I can't get a picture.

I miss you. It was really great seeing you. I hope you are doing well.

-c

II.

What else are you doing this week? Are you spending a lot of time alone? Do you have many friends in Santa Cruz? Did you have many friends you share with your ex?

Have you been to Hat Yai? It is a weird city in Thailand on the border of Malaysia. It is something similar to Bangkok, with the dogs and the heat and the fish sauce, but the people are not as friendly. Singapore is a great city. Very clean and efficient. It is a little sickening as well. Although it has many different cultures, they seem to have all assimilated into one, wearing nothing with a hole, tear, stain, or wrinkle. All are clean shaven and very proper. Before I left Hat Yai, I shaved. Well, actually, I paid fifty baht to be shaved. I thought I would regret it. I actually feel very free and light. Although Thai people are very nice, I felt their apprehension and disapproval of my beard. It was a good move to shave. Plus, it is nice to have a breeze on my face.

I don't know how real you want to get in emails. I did that thing where you write a paragraph and erase it. Then you write another one and you erase that. I will just leave it here.

-c

III.

When i think of you... I am troubled. Scared. Nervous. Anxious. Hoping to be at peace. I want a calm sea that can swallow the earth. I want a wing and a foot. I want air. And I want ground. Can I have both?

Tell me an herb. And make it a good one.

I am supposed to be making magic in my dreams (you told me to) but I can barely sleep.

Ah. I had dreams last night though. Turbulent dreams. You were there. Don't ask me. I don't remember. But I know you were there. Many people were. Making a ruckus. I will try again. To dream and to make magic.

I hope this email finds you well. As always. Thinking of how you may feel about the world. From a window. I can see you watching it turning.

Sleep is just another moment.

yours,

-c

IV.

It is so strange to hang out with people again here in Chiang Mai. It is like my alone time never even happened. But when I think about it, that time was intense. I am glad it is over. I thought about you being here last night with me. I think we would have a lot of fun traveling. You would love it here. But then, anyone would love it here, it is amazing.

When I lay down to sleep at night I think about your legs and your breasts and your lips. You float around, mixed throughout images of my day, and I wake up with the taste of both on my tongue.

-c

V.

I am so warm.

My body is like a little ember sitting in this bed. I may melt the plastic that they left on the mattress. Why did they leave the plastic on the mattress? Why?

I rode twenty five plus miles to a hot spring where people were literally boiling eggs. It was quite a theme. They even had statues of eggs. People would purchase six eggs and an egg basket and put them into the water. There was a billboard that said how long it took for soft, medium, and hard. The spring then flowed through a small canal where you could dip your feet and eventually was funneled into a large pool where we bathed. Sulfur smells like eggs anyway, but I think the fact that hundreds of eggs were boiled in the water a day added to the scent. I sat in the hot water on this hot day for about fifteen minutes. My skin is silky smooth and my hair is thick and fluffy. Then I rode back twenty five plus miles. This was all on a fixed gear, mind you, so my legs are moving the entire time. Needless to say - I'm a bit sleepy.

I have very low expectations of chatting with you tonight. I wish for it but I don't feel that it will happen given the time difference right now and that you are likely asleep in these early morning hours on your side of the planet. How is school? Are you studying hard? What herbs are you learning about?

Time is moving and moving and moving.

I will see you soon.

-c

VI.

It is almost midnight. I am going to sleep well tonight. I remembered some of my dreams last night.

I was in a bicycle accident. It was close to being bad but I was okay. Someone died and I think I had something to do with it. You were standing in a white shirt and blue jean shorts and hiking boots and socks near water and a dock on a pond and there was green, long grass and trees. This is all I remember. Fragments. I am so curious about dreams. I want them. Tonight I want a magical dream. I want to remember it. I will try.

I am going to book my ticket back to the US tomorrow. Still not sure exactly when I am leaving but... I am really looking forward to being with you...

I crave you.

-c

61.

(talks with you)

"I wanted to ask if you would be there when the baby is born."

"Oh wow. Man I don't know about that."

"I know it's a big thing to ask but you're the closest person to me and it would mean a lot."

"Wow... I don't think I can do that."

"Okay… It's okay, I understand."

"How are you?"

"I'm okay. Got a lot going on."

"Yeah."

"You?"

"I'm good."

"You still dating her?"

"Yeah. I mean. I think you could call it that. Thanks for asking."

"How are things going?"

"Good. Intense. I'm not sure really."

"I miss you."

"Yeah. I miss you too."

62.

(poem)

she is now shaped as an outline
laying naked like a tusk on my sleeping pillows
baring obvious truth a body once existed
but i do not own a knife or the hands of a hunter

I was with you when you called him to tell him you were pregnant and he told you he would come take it out for you himself. I was sitting in a chair in your shared two-bedroom apartment in Northampton where you moved right after you came back to Mass, after that night in the hotel and after we smoked that last pill together and after we sat on the floor on that mattress in what would become my shared two-bedroom apartment in Florence. You paced around in front of me with him on the phone. I only knew then that you'd met him while you were working down south and I was on the Cape and that you flew out to see him in California after we separated. You'd had a few days lapse in your birth control and somehow became pregnant. You later told me you became lovers while we were still together and you lived with him down south and I was on the Cape but the rest happened the same way you told it then. I watched you hang up either on him or him on you, and say something like, "I can do it without him." And I answered, "Yes. You got this."

He woke up early and watched her sleep. Her face reminded him of a strawberry. Or maybe just her cheeks and the way they moved into her nose and lips and all blush, pink and dots of freckles like seeds. Or maybe it was just a poem he had written a long time ago about a strawberry and about love and she reminded him of the poem.

He had a headache and he was thirsty from the drink the night before. After a day at the beach where they found an empty inlet and she took off her clothes and just kept her panties on and told him one of her breasts was smaller than the other. They went back to her place and they made some food and drank something strong and started getting silly. They spent the night naked, making sock puppets with her old socks and some buttons. It went on for hours. They also made love and he looked at her breasts and the one that was smaller, he kissed. And throughout the night she was feisty and she pushed him and also pulled him and he felt both how she loved him and also feared him and maybe feared herself. He felt how she loved him and also was repelled by him and maybe repelled by love itself. He felt it all and had no words for it, just feelings. They went to sleep and she said she didn't want to sleep close, that she wanted her own space. But while she was sleeping, she moved close to him and put her skin on his skin.

He watched her. She breathed in and breathed out.

He got up and went to the kitchen. He drank some water. He sat on the couch and opened up his computer. He looked at the screen for a minute, then closed it. He didn't feel right. He put his feet up on the small table in front of him and looked at the way the sun coming in through the window colored his toes and he wanted to stay in that house forever.

Sometime later she woke up and she was thirsty and had a little headache. She got some water and made some toast and sat down near him on the couch. It felt normal in many ways. He had visited her here enough times that he knew it. He knew the smell of the place and the feel of the floor on his bare feet. And he knew her in some ways and also knew nothing. He laid his head on her shoulder. She groaned in irritation and moved away. After she finished her toast she put her legs over his lap and lay down with her head on the arm of the couch. He stroked her legs and asked what she wanted to do.

"I think I need to do some work today."

"Okay."

"So you need to go."

"Okay."

"You're going to go do that hike still?"

"Yeah."

"Want to get some food first?"

"Yeah."

And they went somewhere and got smoothies and they spent some time on a table in the sun and he missed her. He felt the way she was the tide and he a stone, rolling in and rolling out as she pulled and pushed. She kissed him then and told him she would miss him. "I love you."

"I love you too."

And then they were back at her place and he packed up his things. She gave him the little yellow chair for his art table and for his keyboard and because she didn't want it anymore, and he put it in the car next to his backpack and he left and drove north. He felt heavy and ignored it. He thought about his feet and the way the sun from the window colored them. He thought about sock puppets. He thought about strawberries. He thought about freckles and children and toast.

Hours later he called her from the road. He felt bright after having some movement under his body and he missed her. She answered and she was with people and she was laughing with them in between saying hello and how are you. And because he needed a level of reassurance that was not possible to give to another human being and because he felt like she wouldn't offer it even if she could, the setting sun and the dawning night took hold of him. He felt replaced and rejected. He felt angry and he felt small. He didn't say these things but they were felt and she didn't say she needed space but he knew she did. They hung up and he drove but didn't move. He made it to Arcada and got a motel and a couple of beers and called an escort and she answered and they talked and he said he would call her back to set something up but he didn't and masterbated instead. He resolved to be stronger. He resolved to be less needy. He resolved to pretend he didn't love her as much as he did. And he told himself it was going to work out. And he fell asleep a little drunk and looking forward to losing himself in the Redwoods the next day.

65.

(letter to her)

I worry that you feel I am shutting you out. That I have gone. That I am moving away from you. I am not. I just want to give you space. I think you need it from me. And maybe you need it for a while. I don't want you to feel like you are in a relationship or feel burdened or overwhelmed. You should do whatever you need to do and whatever feels right for you. You can't force anything.

I have not left. I am just around the corner. Say my name and I will hear you.

Into the wilderness now. Looking forward to a healing, forest cleanse.

-c

66

I was driving my parents' car because my truck, the one your stepfather built for us, needed a little work after that long drive from Massachusetts a month or so before. It was a bad idea to drive their car to the trail head. Or maybe it was just the roads I had chosen were a bad idea. I didn't know then that I had other options of where to go to start the trail. I had not done much planning, really. I left Arcada in the morning and on my way to the forest station, I picked up a guy hitchhiking. In some ways he reminded me of your stepfather in that he was older and work-colored with sun and you could tell he knew how to fix things and take care of his own. He had been at a casino all night and smelled of booze. He was tired and haggard and wrinkled and smelled of stale cigarettes and I guess I felt some sort of kindred understanding in him. I drove him to a gas station not too far away from, where he said, he could get a ride up to his trailer and I gave him twenty dollars. He just sat there for a minute with his mouth half-gaped and then thanked me, opened the door, hopped out, and went into the gas station. I imagine he bought alcohol or cigarettes or scratch tickets or some combination of those things and I felt good about it. I understood. By the time I got to the forest station my hangover was beginning to show itself. *That's okay,* I thought, *I just need to get into the woods and let this all out of me.*

I got a pass for the backcountry and a tide chart to carry in my pack and was told I had to put my food in bear canisters and they gave me two enormous black, plastic containers. I just nodded and took them with no intention of lugging around two suitcase-sized cans. I had brought rope to hang my food in a bag from a tree. I knew what I was doing. . And then I drove into the woods. A couple hours later I found the peek of the trail where one large truck was parked. I pulled over and put my pass in the window and hid the bear canisters in the trunk. I checked the time on my phone - one PM - and then turned it off. I strapped on my backpack and got on the trail as my hangover began to envelope me.

The first phase of the trail was entirely downhill. So much so that my toes ached after the first mile from being jammed into the foot of my boot. And my hangover was full strength and banging around in my blood and my brains. But I felt free and elevated by the pain that I knew accompanied all release and so I half ran for several miles until I began to hear the crashing of waves and maybe twenty minutes after that the trees fell back and the shore announced itself and I was standing in a little cove facing the Pacific in all its glory and horror and I watched it roaring onto the stony shore and swallowing the land and giving it back. I took off my pack and decided to stay there for the night. I was feeling pretty nauseous. So I set up a simple cover with a tarp and a line running down the middle and staked the corners. I rolled out another tarp on the ground and then my sleeping pad and then my sleeping bag and I curled the top of the bag onto itself so nothing got in before I did, and I went to find some water to pump and some wood to burn. I had at least two, maybe three, hours left of daylight and I was feeling sicker and heavier quickly and needed to get myself set up so I could just let it do its thing.

After I pumped some water from a little creek and collected some wood and built a fire I'd light later, I felt my stomach turn and flip onto itself and for the next couple hours I leaned against a tree with my pants down and held my face in my hands just trying to breathe.

When that was finished and the sun went down, I lit the fire and heated up some water and made some tea from nettles I'd foraged near the stream. I sat there and watched the flames until it was black out and the stars were shining. I pulled my bedroll and sleeping bag out from under the tarp and laid them down near the fire. I got inside my bag and I looked up at the sky and listened to the crashing waves and moving rocks. I didn't think. I just lay there like a piece of the moment, no more and no less significant than the nettle growing along the stream or one of the stones that was being sucked in and spit out by the ocean.

In the morning everything was wet and heavy with ocean breath and fog. I checked the tide chart. It would be an okay time to head out. I packed up and walked down onto the sand. I crossed over the creek where I had pumped water. It spilled down from the mountain where my car sat somewhere high up above and fed itself into the ocean through a trough of large rocks before spreading out and melding with the crashing waves and fist-sized stones.

It was eerie. On one side of me was a cliff, sharp and staggering and looking like one of those cliffs around the edges of the pass from Santa Ynez to Santa Barbara. On the other side, a slowly encroaching sea that roared and panted like a hungry dragon. And in the early morning I saw no human tracks, but I did begin to notice the huge bear tracks that littered the wet sands. And every so often in the line of those tracks a fresh and warm pile of bear dung the size of one of those fucking canisters I had left in the trunk. And being so alone in the midst of such greatness, I began to feel paranoid about the food that was in my pack and these bear tracks that went every which way and this sea that was just waiting to crush me against this rock face and swallow me up.

As the morning went on, I got more comfortable walking near the water where the sand was wetter and easier to hike. And at one point I turned my back to the water and took my bag off and got out some dried fruit out of a side pouch - when I heard a huge crash and I turned around to see the break of a gigantic wave hurling down onto the shore a mere twenty feet from me and rushing toward me with immense fury. I had just enough time to grab my pack and climb up a three-foot rock and brace myself. The sea splashed against the rock and came over it about four inches. It pawed at the sands below where I had just been standing and raked about half a foot of the earth into its mouth before sucking itself back into its greater mass. The tracks I had created were obliterated. I jumped down onto the sand and ran up closer to the rock face before the next wave came in. The tide was rising and I was getting close to an area that could only be traversed at low tide. Which wouldn't happen until the following morning. I looked on the map and saw there was another small creek up ahead before the narrow passage and I imagined there was enough room there to set up a camp. An hour later I found the creek and there was an opening to the mountain where the cliffs tapered off and trees and small shrubs grew. I found an area with flat enough ground and I set up my camp. I didn't bother making the tarp tent this time. I just spent the rest of my day collecting wood so I could make a strong fire and dry my shoes and socks and watch it glow into the darkness.

And it was that night I started thinking about her. After my hangover had run its course and the fear of the sea and the bears and the mud and the boulders had settled itself, what was left was that cold stone in my gut and it made it impossible to get warm. I writhed in my sleeping bag and slept fitfully and dreamed of death. And in the morning I packed up my things and waited for a couple of hours for the tide to be at its lowest and during that time I looked at the ocean and wondered how the fuck I was going to get through this and what the fuck that actually meant and where the fuck I would be once I did. It was a sense of hopelessness that was, in this wild and empty backcountry, grounding and profound and simple and it was not to be escaped.

I got back on the trail when the tide was lowest and for a couple hours ran between sets of waves and stood on tall rocks to wait for the water to pass where the side of the cliff and edge of the water created a thin passage that, even at low-tide, could not be considered entirely safe. But it was helpful and it kept my mind and my heart active and present and after a couple hours the trail lifted up a dozen feet away from the ocean and into a meadow that was beautiful with shin-high grass and low flowers.

Slowly the trail moved further and further away from the ocean through the meadow until I was surrounded by woods and taking switchbacks. The day grew hot and I was low on water and I really wasn't sure I was on the right trail. There were no rivers or creeks to pump from up there. The next camp site was said to have a spring but it could be dry. I could walk right past it. I was feeling a mixture of low-level fear and bull-headed assuredness. I hiked all day until it was evening and the sun was beginning to set. The trail had narrowed and the trees had dropped away and even with the sun setting it was hot and dry but I knew it would also be cold soon and I needed to rest. I thought about lying down right there on the narrow trail. *A little further,* I said to myself.

Half a mile later I found a little trail and a decaying wooden sign. I followed the little trail and it opened up and I saw it was flat and surrounded with low bush. I dropped my pack and got out my flashlight. No spring. I was out of water and thirsty. I shone the light around and half buried in a bush twenty feet away, I saw another sign: *Spring.* I took my bottle and my light and followed the sign and in a few minutes I heard a little trickle of water and in a minute more I saw a pipe jammed into the earth and water, like that from a half open faucet, gently rolling out, clean and clear and feeding a tiny stream where ferns were sprouting. I filled my bottle and drank and noticed the tension then and the fear and they began slipping away as I listened to the sound of that water. The relief I felt almost brought me to tears but it left me with a cold sort of sadness that somehow locked those tears up. So, I just sat there for awhile and sipped water and felt both that I wanted to cry and that there was no way I could.

I set up camp that night in the dark thinking about bears and snakes but feeling confident I was on the right trail. I fell asleep easily, overtaken with fatigue and accomplishment. I wasn't really sure how much hiking I had to do the next day but if I didn't take a wrong trail, I would be back to the car by   late afternoon.

In the morning I didn't leave the camp right away. I walked around drinking water knowing this was the last source I would have for the rest of the hike. I thought about you and the time we went to Maine when we had no money. I think we were eighteen. Somehow I had saved enough to buy us both cheap mountain bikes and a bike rack and we loaded them onto that little Toyota Tercel we shared and headed from the Berkshires up to Bar Harbor; to Acadia National Park. We just camped and rode our bikes around for a week. And at some point I went to a little shop to buy beer and to distract them from asking for an ID, I also bought a lobster and just kept asking questions about how to cook it. The beer was a six pack of blueberry ale and the lobster, we named Lobster Saint Lobster. We went down to the water and took off the rubber bands around his hands and placed him on the rocks. For a while he didn't move. Remember? Like he was stunned and overwhelmed by freedom. But eventually the water pushed him a bit in one direction toward the shore and as it sucked back in the other direction toward the open sea, he shook his tale and went with it. And that was it. He was gone and we drank the blueberry ale and when the week was over we loaded the bikes and went back to Great Barrington and you went to school and I went back to work cutting lettuce. And that was pretty much our life together in those first couple years. Anyway. The woods just beyond the spring up on the King's Range reminded me of the woods in Maine. Just for a moment. Where the ground is covered in brown leaves and the branches are scraggly and sort of reach out to you when you walk by.

I filled my water one last time and left the camp and got back onto the trail. There were trails off the main trail I was following often enough to have me second guess myself and at one point I actually did take the wrong one. It started going downhill away from the ocean and it just didn't feel right. I went back up and sat at the fork for a minute looking at the somewhat useless little pocket map before I decided to keep going on the trail that sat atop the range. I was reassured when I found a six-by-six wooden platform just twenty feet off the trail that was the lookout point for the King's Range. It was epic to see the ocean from that height and that distance and yet to know it so intimately. It was like seeing a wild lover clothed and doing some benign activity like reading a book or driving a car and knowing that just beneath that is death and birth and darkness and light but from this distance she looks, simply, pretty. I stood there for a minute with my pack on. I could have stayed longer - forever, maybe - but I felt the pull of comfort and turned away from that grandeur and kept on. Finally, I reached the trailhead I had come in on. My first thought was, *I hope the fucking car turns on*. It did. And this time I didn't drive back the way I had come in but rather continued out the other direction on the off-chance it was easier to traverse. And it was.

67.

(poem)

i took the bed into my arms
to smell you
i painted my face at night
and by myself i danced sometimes
to dark music

68

A couple months after we separated I was lying in bed and you called. You wanted to come over. My housemate, who both loved and feared women as much as I did, told me it was a bad idea by rubbing his beard and lifting his eyebrows and looking at the floor. It was dark out and I was in bed. I watched the headlights of your car through the square windows. I heard your car turn off and your door close. I felt my heart moving. You knocked and I opened the door or maybe I opened the door before you knocked, and in the darkness and in the glow from other homes' little windows, you were backlit. I couldn't see your features but you glowed a bit with an orange outline. We hugged and your body felt smaller than usual. We didn't say much that night. You slipped inside my room and wanted to cuddle so we lay down under the covers and I held you for a while. And I felt the warmth there. And I felt the darkness outside. And I felt the way you arched yourself into me and began moving. And you turned your head and pressed your nose into my neck and slid your hands down my pants. You moved on top of me and didn't kiss me much. I came on my stomach and you left. I lay in my bed and thought about ghosts and shadows. And I felt a torch of shame and fear ignite in the belly of that darkness.

A couple days later the tall, older woman from the bar messaged me a sexy picture of herself in a bathtub covered in bath bubbles and a caption that said, "guess who I'm thinking about." And I wrote her back and I told her I was sorry and that I might get back together with my wife. She felt badly and said she really hoped things worked out for me. I went on for a few more weeks like that, wondering how I would tell you about this older woman and feeling I had destroyed any chance we had. I was lost in shame and being lost in shame allowed me to focus on something other than the reality that we would never be together again and that you had no intention of trying.

I asked if you would go to therapy with me and hired a woman recommended by a friend who was small and sharp and kind and told us we could have any relationship we wanted. She told us that all kinds of relationships existed and it was up to us to determine how we wanted to create it. It didn't seem to change anything, but I felt hopeful that you came and felt like maybe if we just did more of these and maybe if we just took it slowly and maybe if I changed - if I could just get my shit together, make more money, go to the gym, compliment you more, stop masterbating, go back to school, get a career job, sit in an office. If I could stop getting jealous, stop telling people to fuck off when I drive, keep my head down, keep my head up, walk straight, run, find our lost dog, bring your step-father back to life. If I could unfuck that woman, take the pills out of our bodies, and go back to the time we were sixteen in the backseat of that car and the moon was blasting and I took your hand in mine for the first time. If I could go back there and tell you we need to be careful - that this shit can break if we don't take care of it - then maybe, it would be okay.

But the reality of our separation and its permanence did eventually settle across my skin. And at some point I stopped caring. I took everything I needed to feel and process and integrate and I put it in a box and I didn't open it up until I could do it in the colors of other women where the things didn't change, just the hue, and take them out and pretend they had to do with this one and that one and had nothing to do at all with you or even with me.

69

The second year he went to Thailand, he went straight to Chiang Mai. Well. After briefly going to Bangkok to find the small girl in Soi Cowboy who put her hands over her mouth in surprise. She stopped dancing on the go-go bar and came down when he motioned for her. She was happy and he could feel it. He was more confident and maybe a little stronger and although he wasn't planning on drinking, after he paid the bar fees and she went up the backstairs and came back, she took his hand again and led him to the little stand outside with the homemade whiskey and ordered two - so he drank. They went back to his place in the same hotel but on a different floor and they made love. It felt so similar as the previous year but something had changed and he couldn't put his finger on it. He thought she was a little removed maybe, or hardened perhaps. It was subtle and encircled the evening's edge. In the morning she was quick to leave and he felt, he'd probably never see her again. The next day he took the sleep train up to Chiang Mai where you defecate right on the tracks from a hole cut out in the floor just below the squat toilet. He slept in a small bed that pulled down from the ceiling in what could only be compared to a womb or maybe a coffin, rocking and swaying over the tracks in rough and gentle vibration.

He arrived at the Chiang Mai train station and took a tuk tuk to a small hotel along the Ping River across the bridge from the large outdoor market of Muang Mai. He had stayed there for one night before and somehow the old, leathered Thai man who took care of the grounds remembered him by his last name and took him to the bar area to get him checked in. The bar sat twenty feet off the river. A structure of twenty feet by thirty feet with a roof and no walls and a plank floor, empty except for the bartender who also acted as the desk clerk and cleaning person. She was a beautiful Thai woman with long, black hair that played below the crest of her ass and she was slightly plump and motherly with a genuine smile, flirtatious eyes.

"You can sit. I can get your key and check your room. Okay?"

"Yeah that's great."

"I remember you. You stay here last year, right?"

"Yeah. Good memory."

"Haha no." And he remembered that Thai people don't generally exchange compliments and don't really know what to do with them when they are given, even if they are just simple things almost built into Western ways of speaking. But she did smile and he saw dimples in her full cheeks. "You want beer?"

"No. Thank you." And she left to check on the room.

He dropped his bag on a chair and sat in another and looked out at the Ping River. A vast and dirty thing with subtle swiftness collecting and swallowing the water from a few dozen tributaries which drained from wild mountains and rice fields and township wastewater. A fisherman stood in the water up to his knees with his pants rolled up casting a net that floated in the air and spread out and then sunk into the water. Another man sat nearby, barefoot, smoking next to three fishing poles with lines extended into the center of the river. Some plastic bits collected in tufts of grass that sprouted in the mud shore and a dead fish or two floated on the surface of the water.

"Okay. All ready." The beautiful bartender handed him the keys and told him the room number. He picked up his bag and found his room. It was on the second floor and through the back window, he could see the empty parking lot of a large bar that hosted DJ'd parties over the weekend. The room was simple, with a bed and a small desk with no drawers and a little closet and a small wet bath with brown tile. The room itself had an orange feel to it, not only because the walls were orange but because the light found itself in the room through a path of leaves and curtains that seemed to strip away the yellow and the bright and left a soft glow like a salt lamp. He took off his shoes and lay down on the bed and smiled and felt good.

A week later he would make love to a girl he met the day before in the orange light of that room. She would be soft and perhaps a little shy but embodied and open and strong. Her long, brown hair would flow over the bed and her face, in pleasure, would lose itself and he would watch it happen and want for it again. Her skin would be white and her eyes brown and hazel. She would tell him things about her boyfriend back home in Canada but not much other than she wasn't really feeling it anymore, or at least, also wanted other experiences and she just needed to give herself permission to have them. They would take a shower together using the small, instant, electric shower and wouldn't fall in love but he would love her and he would feel good and he would sleep deeply that night in that room that held onto its orange glow even in darkness.

The second time I went to Thailand I hosted a series of events. I told you about it, but I don't think you ever really knew the details. Really, at the time, it was just a way for me to make sure I wouldn't be alone. But it was surprisingly successful in a way I couldn't have foreseen. Thirty or so people came from different parts of the world. All were kind and fun and excited about life and just wanted to be excited about life with other people who were excited about life. It was, in a lot of ways, the first thing I created since us that was truly my own and different from anything I'd done before. It wasn't artwork. It wasn't poetry. It wasn't building something or fixing something. It was created from something else I didn't know I had. And maybe I didn't know I had that ability until we separated and I died a little, which made room for something else to be born.

I created an event or two each day for something like a week. They were mostly things I had done the year before, so it wasn't difficult for me. But it was a strange feeling to have a group of people show up to be led by me because I was still learning to lead myself.

We rode bikes from Chiang Mai to Sankampaeng Hot Springs where everyone had a shit bike and one person rode without shoes. We dipped our feet in the near-boiling water that corraled itself down a three-foot, man-made trough where, just above us, Thai families cooked eggs in little baskets that hung in the water and beyond them, a geyser of roiling water shot into the air.

We hiked up Suthep Mountain on Pilgrim's Trail, used by monks for who knows how many years, where old trees are honored with strips of orange monk robes tied around the trunks. We spent time at Wat Palad, the first temple, with statues of elephants and dragons and tigers and looks out over all of Chiang Mai from an opening in the trees where a small creek flows over slippery rocks. Then we went up to Doi Suthep where everything is gold and rang the bells and became part of the swarm of Thai and Chinese tourists.

We also just spent time together eating and laughing. I had rented a three-bedroom house for the event near the Ping River and close to the hostel where I was staying. A few people were staying there with me and because I was learning about the balance of taking care of myself and taking care of others, I opted for the one bedroom that wasn't really a bedroom at all - a small space on the first floor near the kitchen with a cot and a mattress that hurt. One night when everyone was asleep I snuck out of the front door and quietly pulled my bike out from behind the gate and rode to a 7-Eleven and bought a Chang beer and a package of fried seaweed and found a silent street and sat down on the curb and drank and ate and watched a white dog sniffing around bags of trash.

We would often come back to the house I rented. All thirty or so of us would spread out on the tables outside or just in the kitchen. One night we were playing music and someone started dancing and then others were dancing and then I found myself dancing. A woman who was married and was there with her husband and her three-year-old son caught me off guard. Her hips and her breasts and the way she moved them, circular and rhythmic, I couldn't help but watch and she looked at me and I looked at her and her eyes told me she wanted me to watch, and it terrified me.

The next day, the woman and her husband gave a talk on relationships. A girl heard about the event from something I had posted online and showed up. She was a young Canadian with small plugs in her earlobes and a boxy but curvy body. It was a couple hours before the talk and everyone was hanging around the tables outside or making food in the kitchen and she sat down next to me and asked if I was the organizer and I said I was and we chatted.

When it was time for the talk, we all went into the room that was supposed to be my bedroom and everyone sat on the floor and this young Canadian with white skin and her eyes brown and hazel, sat right next to me and our legs were maybe an inch apart. The woman and her husband, who I had been getting to know over the previous few days and felt a great love and appreciation for, stood facing us all and shared about their relationship, which was open and dynamic and inspiring and beautiful. They shared about needs and desires and multiple partners and asking for what you want. And they took questions and the young Canadian asked if it was okay to explore with other people even though she had a boyfriend and they answered something like, "That is really up to you but if you are not getting your needs met, you deserve to at least question that," and I think that was the permission she needed and soon our feet were touching and her thigh was thick and cream colored and warm against my own.

We stayed in my room and talked and faced each other and played with each other's fingers as everyone slowly cleared out and I shut the door. We sat on that little uncomfortable bed and kissed and took our clothes off and she lay down and I lay on top of her. Her breasts were small and her nipples were a dark, walnut brown and her lips and mouth were wet and pink and red. Her breath smelled like juniper and I thought of her in a cabin in the woods above Vancouver where she said she was from. We made love and she stayed with me until morning in that little, uncomfortable bed. The next day we had our last event and I packed up my things and moved back to the hostel just a few blocks away. She met me there in the early evening and we spent some hours together. Then she took a bus up to Pai and I stayed in my orange room and thought about relationships.

Paris, France is a shitty place if you are looking for friendship or kindness or even conversation, especially if that conversation is in anything but unaccented Parisian French. It is also beautiful and crisp and old and clean with side streets made of blocks that wind through dense multi-storied buildings with shops on the first level, all pink-beige and off-white. You can walk for a few blocks and get lost and ask for help and be ignored or you can stay on the same street and find a park that opens up to green grass and short shrubs and tall trees. You can go to the Eiffel Tower and just look at it because the line of tourists is nauseating. You can buy fresh roasted chestnuts from Arabs that have collected them from the street, fallen from the trees, and cooked them in little handmade stoves with glowing coals. You can buy baguettes and small cups of oily espresso anywhere and no matter where you go or what time of day it is, you will never get away from the exhale of a cigarette.

He took a flight from LAX to Paris and she picked him up. It was early in the morning there and he was awake and she was waking up. She got out of the car and they hugged tightly and kissed. He wanted to kiss more. He wanted passion. But she wanted to get in the car and so they did. Then she started driving. It was a forty-five minute trip from the airport to her family home in the suburbs and the entire drive felt like they were in one long car chase scene. On the highway she drove two feet behind the car in front of her until it pulled to the other lane and she sped up to the next car and drove two feet behind that one. On the slower roads, she didn't stop at stop signs or slow down at roundabouts; she just plowed through, her body and his flying against one side of the car and then the other. The entire time she was asking him how he was and how the flight was and pointing things out along the way. "That's the rock climbing gym you can use if you move here."

He was good at being calm when he probably shouldn't have been. And he had been in wild rides before and knew that the best thing was just to relax. His ex-wife drove a little crazy too. Not quite this crazy but it was up there. She got it from her mother who was half-blind and a bit psychotic and was the most insane driver he had ever experienced. Once she did a u-turn on an off ramp using the sidewalk as a lane and when a car blew its horn she blew her horn and cursed him to Hell and back. And this is when he said from the backseat of her car, "are you crazy?!

You're the one that almost drove right into him from the curb!" He was truly afraid and she just recoiled into femininity and laughed and dismissed him and that is probably when he learned it was best to just lean back into the seat, relax, and accept whatever fate has in store.

Finally she slammed on the brakes and said, "we're here."

The yard was messy and overgrown and small. An overly sweet vinegar smell hung in the air and soon he found a fifteen-foot tree loaded with Asian pears as big as the heads of newborns. There must have been thirty on the ground, mostly half-rotting and fermenting. The house was two stories, rock or cement block or brick and gray.

"That's where we could live if you move here." She pointed to a one-story building in the corner of the yard a bit larger than a shed with stone path leading to an off-white door, dirt speckled at the bottom from rainfall.

They went into the house through the garage which was also the basement which was also where her mother housed her obsession with clothes. In the unfinished and dimly lit space he could see rows and rows of haphazard clothing, racks stuffed with fur coats and gowns in plastic wrap and pantsuits and purses with rhinestones and purses with glitter and purses with gold. They went up a set of unfinished stairs and opened a door and went into the kitchen just to the left where a woman sat on a barstool chewing on something. Her back was to them as they entered. She was wearing a black and gold blouse and black slacks and black socks and her hair was black and shimmering in a sort of mushroom shape.

She turned to them vaguely and he was ready with a smile and ready to hug her and ready to present himself. He had cut his hair and shaved and bought a nice sweater and wore blue pants with no stains, not even one, and nice shoes and fuck, he even had a belt on. But the woman didn't really acknowledge him and instead began speaking Mandarin and gesturing around to them both, mostly to her daughter, but definitely including him as if he had been coming and going for years and that this conversation was just a continuation of one they'd been having.. *Yes. Something else important has come to mind and so what do you think about that?* Her gestures said this and the harshness of the language felt like broken glass being thrown at his face.

"Mom, speak English." But Mom didn't speak English. She just stood up and moved around the kitchen putting things away here and there and continued throwing broken glass at his face. He heard feet on stairs and then from around the corner a man entered the kitchen. "Dad, this is my boyfriend."

"Hello," the man said.

"It's nice to meet you." He reached his hand out and smiled. The man looked down at the extended hand and with great effort lifted his own hand to take it. His hand felt cold and wet like paper that was full of water. Then the man sat down at one of the barstools around the kitchen counter island. He saw death all around this man and he thought about his ex-wife's stepfather the days before he died and the way the skin turns yellow and - every. single. thing. is. an. excruciating. effort. This man in jeans and a polo shirt tucked in and his black hair combed but unkempt was not only carrying death around his neck like a chain, but he was also slouched and compressed by the weight of a great burden and it was clear at once what that great burden was.

"Mom," she said to the woman with the mushroom hair. "Can you just say hello." He felt bad for her. She was clearly embarrassed about her mother and not because it was unusual behavior but because it seemed quite normal. He was off-put but he'd also seen a lot of unusual behavior from mothers of lovers. Nonetheless, he found himself remembering something someone had said in a movie: look at the body of the girl's mom - that's what she's gonna look like in thirty years. He wasn't so interested in the body, but he did find himself wondering about the personality. He quickly put those thoughts away, though. She wasn't like this woman and he wasn't like this man and they had bigger plans and she didn't seem to be all that interested in jackets and gowns and purses.

After an awkward thirty minutes or so she led him upstairs to her room. She had never really lived anywhere else. It didn't surprise him all that much because he knew that lots of other cultures lived together until they were married and sometimes long after that. He sat on her bed and she lay down next to him and he lay down and they faced each other. They hadn't seen one another in real life for a couple months. Her face was oval, white and her lips were large, full, brown, purple and pink. They kissed and he pulled her thin body into his. He wanted her. They took off their clothes and made love. She was tight and smooth and her breath smelled like air and her long black hair fell down her back and over her face and over his as she moved on top of him and they looked at each other and smiled. It was good to see her. It wasn't amazing, he thought, but he was tired of amazing. Or. Passion that was chaotic. The stuff that is there one minute and then gone. Drugs. He was tired of getting high on women that left him or he wanted to leave. He wanted good. He wanted decent and doable and regular and repeatable and something sturdy and steady and something to build a life on top of.

A couple hours later they went to a farmer's market. They bought greens and cucumbers and figs from Spain and twenty dollar cherry tomatoes that tasted like candied strawberries. They packed the food in some crates in the back seat and on the way back to her parents' house she almost ran over a couple of people crossing the street and she slammed on the brakes. The crates flew into the backs of their seats and the figs and the tomatoes and cucumbers and greens broke their bodies into one another. She apologized and he said it was all good and thought maybe this was something they could work on over time. Everyone has their stuff.

When they got back to her parents' house they left the crates in the car because they were going to an Airbnb in Paris center. They had rented a space for his visit away from her parents' house - for obvious reasons. When they went into the house her parents were in the kitchen speaking Mandarin and she said, "we're back," and they both spoke to her in Mandarin at the same time and she spoke back in Mandarin as he stood there feeling increasingly uncomfortable in his blue slacks and stupid belt which was completely pointless as the slacks themselves were, in fact, just a little too tight to begin with and he felt a desire to pull them away from the ever-mounting infringement on his genitals, but he held off.

She turned away from her parents and asked, "Can you help my dad?"

"Yeah, of course."

The man looked at him with deep concern and anxiety and then turned and walked out the front door. He followed him out the door and around the side of the house where the smell of shit was overwhelming.

"Sewer problem." The man pointed to a circle cut into the concrete foundation the size of a manhole. There was a pipe running down from the house into the hole. Knowing what he knew about construction, the setup didn't make much sense. The older man hit the pipe with his hand and worried. He stood watching, completely unsure of how to be helpful. After fifteen minutes of this there was a knock at the gate. They walked over and opened it and two overweight men in overalls and thick, matted jackets came in and the dying man spoke French to them and gestured around the side of the house. The men came around to the side of the house and laughed and covered their noses and said something in French to him and he smiled and had no idea what was said. The men went out through the gate and came back with some tools and went to work and after thirty minutes or so the job was done.

At about that time she came through the front door with a swollen roller-bag and up and back down with some clothes on hangers. He helped her load them into the car, careful not to place the tails of the hanging clothes in the lettuce and cucumbers and figs and tomatoes. Soon they were driving into Paris and soon they were finding their Airbnb and soon they were watching some shows on Netflix.

In the morning she went to work and he went out walking. He bought a baguette and an espresso and eventually found himself in a park where, when looking for a bathroom, he found a tennis court with a fifteen-foot wooden wall and at the the top of the wall was a graffiti stencil in black of a man fucking a woman doggie style and he thought of the conversation they'd had in the car on the way to the Airbnb. He had shared about ass play and she had said maybe once a year, like on his birthday. She had also said that she never really liked oral sex. Giving or receiving. But she had done some work around it and felt like it was an okay thing to do. He doubted she had ever had an orgasm. He would ask her soon. It would be good to talk about all of this more deeply. It was all good though. He didn't need wild sex. He didn't need to go down on her every day. He didn't need to be entirely met there. He wanted a child and he wanted a family and he wanted a partnership and a life that was not lonely.

Later, when they went back to her parents' house before she drove him to the airport, he helped her bring her bags upstairs and opened her closet to hang some of her clothes. The closet was stuffed with haphazard clothing, fur coats, and gowns in plastic wrap and pantsuits and purses with rhinestones and purses with glitter and purses with gold.

73.

(talks with you)

"I fucking hate you."

74

I said something terrible to you before our divorce. I'm sorry. It was true in that moment and for those parts of me but I know it wasn't necessary to say. Not like that anyway.

I flew in from California. I landed in Hartford, Connecticut and took a train to Springfield, Massachusetts and you picked me up and brought me to Belchertown. The house looked tired. There was a hole in the roof that I never fixed from that big storm the day before I went to the Cape to live without you, not knowing I was going to live without you. I was busy that day so I just took a chainsaw to the branch that was sticking through the top of the cabinets in the kitchen and dangling six feet over the gutters outside and chopped it up. The hole in the roof was pretty clean and not too big, maybe four to six inches. I cut a piece of plywood and wrapped a tarp around it and nailed it over the hole and put another chunk of tarp over that and tucked it under a row of asphalt shingles so the water wouldn't catch too much. I was thinking it would work for the rest of the winter and I would give it a proper fix in the spring.

But spring was death for me and I ended up just leaving it, knowing one way or another this house was going to disappear from my life. The tenants never complained but I guessed it might have been leaking, at least a little bit into the attic. I got out of the car and started up the Ford Ranger. It hadn't been started in a few months. You had to go back to work or something so you left. I hugged you, you got into your car and pulled away.

The tenants came out of the house and Newton, the dog, ran around the yard and smelled my shoes.

"Hey buddy," the girl said to me. My old math tutor. The one I never kissed. "How are you?"

"I'm good." I wasn't.

"It's good to see you," her boyfriend said and stepped forward to give me a hug.

"You too, man." It was. And I hugged him.

They went back inside and I watched Newton defecate just beyond the driveway where we had planted some Asian roses years before. Then I turned around and went into the garage.

It was a single car garage with a short peaked roof and a bit deeper than most. After I had moved out of Florence I moved into that garage. I planned to renovate it into a studio apartment. I ran new rafters along the roof to extend the width and put in insulation. I built a wall with a door in the front so when you lifted the garage door you'd see an area of storage maybe six feet deep and would have to enter through another door to access the studio. I built a platform on the concrete slab of a floor and ran plumbing from the basement through a small window nestled into the garage and had just enough room for a four-inch ABS and a couple of flex tubing lines and I hooked up a toilet and shower plumbing. I had started tiling the walls of the shower. I had a toilet and sink that worked. I had a bed with a ladder to it that suspended itself in the rafters. It needed a little more electrical work and it needed a floor and it needed drywall but it was more than habitable and although I was proud of what I had done, I had no intention of finishing.

I was shedding this place.

Anything I thought I could sell, I pulled outside and took pictures of. Anything I wanted to keep, I made a pile of. Anything that was trash, I stuffed into the little four-by-five wood shed that had been leaking for a few years, thinking it would be easy for someone to just stick a jack under the shed and wheel it into a dumpster. I spent the rest of the day doing this. It was cold and damp and sad but I wasn't allowing myself to feel the sadness, I just focused on the task at hand and kept returning to the idea of letting go and shedding and getting away and yes, I thought about her a lot. I thought about returning to her in her little one-bedroom in Santa Cruz. I thought about making love to her. I thought about having children with her. And I felt itchy with it all, knowing I had to wait until our court date and knowing I had a lot of shit to do before then and a lot of it had to include you and I was angry about it. I was angry at you, actually. But that, too, was something I was denying and it was festering.She had asked me at some point how I felt about it all and how I felt about you and how I felt about our separation and I said, "I'm all good," and, "it was good, it was for the best, I'm good," and she told me she didn't think that was totally honest and she asked if I was angry at you. And I guess no one had asked me that before or maybe someone had, but the weight of it from her sat inside me and gave me permission to feel. Yes, I was angry. I was really fucking angry. And I wonder if she had asked me if I was sad, would I have felt sad.. I think the truth is, I felt sad all the time but I never really felt the anger.

That night I slept in the garage and I thought about the nights that the small girl from Turkey slept in that bed with me and said she didn't mind at all that the place was half built. She didn't mind at all about not having a shower. She didn't mind at all about having to climb down a ladder to go pee in the middle of the night. She was sweet. There's no doubt about that. I wondered if I might run into her while I was back in town. I didn't.

The next day passed in a blur of cleaning and mowing and lifting and scraping until the evening when I was to meet you and our old friends in Amherst. Our friends were a couple that we had shared a lot of history with that loved us as a couple but were perhaps figuring out their relationship with us as individuals and down the road would decide we didn't make the cut. After that, I was going to go to Turners Falls and stay with you there in one of the two empty units and help you clean out whatever needed to be cleaned out from the basement and the attic.

As I drove to meet you I didn't know my anger was with me. But I think it was sitting in the passenger's seat just waiting.

75

Before I left to Thailand for the first time, I went over to your place in Northamptom. I had just broken up with my girlfriend and although I was sad about it, I also felt I had made the right decision and parts of me were resolute and stone strong. You were a few months pregnant and showing. It felt good to talk to you about my process and what I was looking forward to. We had sex. It was the first time we'd had sex since we separated. It felt normal, and also different. Partly because you had a baby growing inside of you and partly because I was sober and partly because you were becoming a stranger to me and also a new friend. I spent the night and in the morning I was ready to go and you wanted to have sex again and you opened up the covers for me and said, "come here," and I have to tell you, I didn't want to. I felt sad and a little sick and maybe the love I had felt for my now ex-girlfriend was weighing on me and maybe it was parts of me building defenses against you and maybe it was just the epic dissolution of the set up.

We did have sex again and you commented that it was funny that I just had break-up sex with my ex-wife even though we were not technically divorced yet, but I understood what you meant and I did think that it was funny - in a sort of horror flick comedy way, and I felt a heavy shadow and a few demon faces hiding there and we hugged and I said goodbye. I put that darkness in my pocket and I flew to California for a week for Christmas and I saw her and

I started making the transfer of love and pain and loneliness and abandonment and passion and life-building away from you and onto her because I think it was easier that way, and maybe it was also because I had always loved her in a way I never loved you.

I imagine this is at least true in that we never love anyone the same way, do we? And I think that is partly what makes each ending and new beginning so painful. When it changes and we can't get to it like we want to get to it and can't be in it like we need to be in it and we can't just lie down and cuddle it to sleep anymore and we have to figure out how to walk near it or never talk to it again or watch it grow someone else's child.

76.

(poem)

you are the closest thing to death i know
when my hand touches your face and freckles
dance over my fingers like lightning on the snow

77

One night I went to her mom's house in Los Olivos. I was wearing this shirt my dad gave me. It was a button-up purple thing with red in it. I can't explain it, really, but it looked good. It always looked good. It could hang on a hanger or on a random dude and it just had this vibe to it; something sort of Native American meets docker meets I-don't-give-a-fuck-poet-in-the-woods. Yeah, I said it's hard to explain but you get it. I felt good. Not quite Native American meets docker but definitely some I-don't-give-a-fuck and even a little poet-in-the-woods. But I also had this I-want-to-marry-this-girl-and-make-babies-with-her thing going on, and if she didn't know it, her mom definitely did.

The door opened and she was there and her mom was too and they were very sweet and smiling and they were both similar and very different. I liked her mom a lot. She worked in the office at my high school where we'd both gone. Recently I'd gone over to her house and knocked on the door just like this and I'd brought some veggies and made her dinner. That night her mom had opened a bottle of wine and I had some like it was no big deal and we'd sat at her table, just the two of us, and talked. She'd told me some things about her daughter. They were things I knew already but hearing them from her was confirming. "She sleeps a lot sometimes," she said. "She can sleep fourteen hours when she is home. No problem." And, "she is cautious with love." I guess, to be honest, I didn't know about the sleeping thing.

This night was different. I gave her a hug and I felt her body and I both relaxed and stiffened. Then I hugged her mom and we smiled at one another. I went inside and they closed the door. There were two others there. A man and woman, older. The woman came up to me and got right in my face and put her hand on my shoulders and said, "oh I can't believe it." And she hugged me. She was a teacher I had in high school; the type who had a sort of bond with everyone. She was sweet and also a little irritating and definitely presumptuous, but it was good to see her and good to be seen. Then I met her husband - I liked him a lot. He was solid and kind and I could tell he dealt with her shit very well. He had taken a sort of backseat, Zen approach to her exuberance and drama and seemed to find it all amusing and I could tell, he loved her to death.

We all sat around the table and ate and drank wine from one of the vineyards right around the corner and at some point, my old teacher asked me about my writing and I told her I wasn't sure about my writing. "I want to write more," I said and, "I'm also doing other things which I enjoy but I don't think are long-term things, like handyman work and construction and house painting." She then launched into how I could write a poem about changing a door knob and how I had to use what was around me to create. I just nodded and noted how old she was and thought her mind was fading and she was still trying to hold onto it or onto something that just wasn't there anymore. Or maybe it was just that I was a grown man now and I never liked people telling me what I should do - especially around my writing. Her husband just leaned back in his chair and smiled at me like he got it and that took the sting out.

Dinner ended. It was dark out. We went out, she and I. We drove in her Subaru through Los Olivos and crossed 154 and onto Figueroa Mountain Road that winds into Los Padres National Forest and we parked before the road starts climbing, right before that old Neverland property. We just pulled off right there on the road into this dirt patch that led to a padlocked gate blocking the entrance to a flat field with some farming equipment, silent and sleeping in the moonlight. She got into the passenger's seat and we pushed the seat back as far as it could go and I crawled down below her and took her pants off and put my face between her legs. We were there for maybe an hour and not one car went up the mountain and not one car came down.

We went back to her mom's where my truck was parked and in the darkness where the red peppercorn trees were hanging low, we kissed goodnight and before I drove back to Santa Barbara, she asked how the yellow chair she gave me was doing. "It's perfect," I told her. And I left and went back to my little studio and I felt like I needed to make a move, like I needed to do something, that I couldn't just stay in this strange interim with her. I felt like I needed to set a line for her to cross. I needed to stop going to her. I needed her to come to me. So a couple days later, I called her and I told her I didn't think I could do this in a healthful way anymore. I was attached to her and I was in love with her and I needed more and if I couldn't have that then maybe I just needed to take a step back.

She was surprised but also understanding and when I lay in bed at night weeks later and thought about the conversation I realized, she was relieved. I believed she would come to me. I believed I had created a setup that would allow her to acknowledge our relationship and our love and I believed she would have an awakening of sorts and that she would send me a text that would say, "I miss you. I need you in my life."

But the days turned into weeks and I realized she was, in fact, cautious and perhaps, stubborn. But more painful than that was trying to understand that what I felt for her was not what she felt for me and this thing I had been creating since I was fourteen was still playing itself out. And, of course, these things start when we are much younger, when we first feel the bite of dismissal and the fangs of rejection but that is a different story. The story I kept thinking about was the day after she had led me into those pea fields and I had fallen in love with her right then and there. I assumed she would want to be my girlfriend but she didn't. She just said, "no. I don't want that." And I had been chasing redemption ever since because parts of me could not accept that what I felt was one-sided. It couldn't be. But what we do and how we react and what we want and what we need and what keeps us up at night and what repels us - I slowly began to accept that those things can be very different.

And through this pain of losing and missing and loneliness and am-I-good-enough and no-I'm-not, I processed you through her and I believe these were different things but also flowed into the same river; a river I watched from a bridge I was still building between a land of trauma and one of health. I could see exactly how far I had to go and to be honest with you, I just wasn't ready to be there yet.

78.

(poem)

she called
to see if i was a man yet
i told her
i was not
she said
she would call back another time to check
maybe
that is
if things didn't change

later
in the night
i lain open
eyed staring at the tousle of leaves
from the octopus tree
and the stars
beyond
i thought to myself
wait
i am a man

i fell asleep
hoping she would call
in the morning
i never heard
from her again

79

He was playing pool in Amherst with a couple of friends and his very soon-to-be ex-wife after cleaning out the house in Belchertown all day. He hadn't seen his friends in a while. They used to all go out together. Not quite on double-dates but something like that. They had also all used to break up pills together, though the girl couldn't handle it so well, so it was mostly the three of them. They were both from the Berkshires and he had known the guy for a while and his girlfriend he'd met more recently, although everyone who grew up in the Berkshires overlaps. He didn't grow up in the Berkshires, but he lived there with his soon-to-be ex-wife long enough and young enough to have connections in a different sort of way than people who move there later in life. Because of this, he knew *of* her for much longer than he actually knew her.

So he was playing pool upstairs at the recently-opened and newly-renovated High Horse, right on the main street. And he was drinking and he was getting drunk and he was getting rowdy and loud and this fucking thing in his pocket, this darkness, was starting to glow.

Outside they went into the small pizza place with all the different pizzas and the line out the door and if you hadn't been there before you wouldn't have any idea how to order and the people serving you the pizza are all rude and there was a girl there. She was a young college student with brown hair and white skin and she was lean and sweet and sort of dumb and he hit on her and told her she was beautiful and she just lit up. And he did this in front of his soon to be ex-wife and in front of his friends and it wasn't meant to be a show for them but it probably felt that way. He just had the fire in him and that fucking glow in his pocket was becoming hot and itchy and he had to do something, had to move something, had to reach out into the world and make sure he was being seen and this girl saw him.

Then they left and went outside where his friend rolled a cigarette and took some puffs and the girls chatted like they used to chat and his friend said to him, "Man, you need to chill out," and he sort of laughed but he was also serious. And he said, "I'm good, bro," and he went back into that pizza shop and he got that girl's number.

Then they all went up to Turners Falls to stay the night in one of the empty units at the two-family home that was about to become entirely hers. His friends had recently moved to NYC and were up visiting family and so they stayed in one of the bedrooms and he stayed in the other with his soon to be ex-wife. And that fucking thing in his pocket was burning a hole in his flesh. And that's when he said it. It was surrounded in other words and other actions and probably sadness that came close to crying but recoiled into anger and it came out at her like a knife and it was meant to cut.

But she still held the covers open for him. And he still lay down with her. And they still fell asleep together with her growing belly resting against his curled back.

80

After he broke up with her, she locked herself in his bathroom for a couple hours. It was dark out. He pulled a pillow next to the door and lay down with his head on it. He let her know he was there. And so he waited.

He knew he couldn't move to France. It wouldn't be right. It wasn't France so much. And it definitely wasn't moving. It was all the subtle things that added up. All the subtle things that at another time in his life may have gone unnoticed. It wasn't that he was pessimistic. He wasn't searching for this shit. But he was open. Man. He was so open and so willing to do what needed to be done to create the next phase of life and was ready to receive and ready to give and ready to build. But yeah, he was suspicious of others and he was suspicious of himself. And he was paying attention to the subtleties now and parts of him were taking notes and doing math and at some point the equation equaled *no go*.

After a couple hours she came out of the bathroom and she was not crying. In fact, she even smiled when he asked if she was okay. And whatever work she had done to right herself had left her half-there and cold and strange and he felt her alien, even to herself.

She still had a few days left in her visit and they slept next to one another in that small closet with no doors where his thin mattress was laid down and that yellow chair sat against the opposite wall. And when New Year's Eve came she told him she wanted to make love. "Yes," he said. But he also wanted to make sure she was okay and he also wanted to make sure she knew he was not going to change his mind. And she said she understood and it was okay, she just wanted to and it didn't have to be a big deal and so they made love and she was on top of him and beautiful and slender like the black bamboo that grew outside his door next to the octopus tree, tall and thin and impossible to break by hand. It felt good to be with her. And they did good things together for the remainder of her trip. But he couldn't help but count the minutes until they would depart.

Finally it came. They took the train from Santa Barbara to LA and a car to LAX and she boarded a plane to France and he boarded a plane to Thailand for the second time. She'd been planning to come and meet him for a week or so, but not anymore. It was an odd transition and he felt it, but when he arrived in Thailand, he felt the sun and he knew how to catch a driver and where to go. He checked into a sweet little hostel along the Ping River which he watched while waiting for his room to be ready and felt free and unburdened and he loved himself a little bit more than before.

(talks with men)

"Well, you know, my mom wasn't really into my dad right away. I mean, he just kept pursuing her and eventually she... you know... got married and had my sister and me."

"Hmm. Do you think she just needed your dad to pursue her? Like - what do you think would have happened if your dad hadn't pursued her?"

"I don't know. But. The way they talk about it, I get the feeling my mom wasn't that into him. He just kept at it and at some point she... saw him."

"You think I should do that?"

"If you love her. Why not?"

"Because it's painful."

"Yeah. But what else are you going to do?"

"Let it go."

"Yeah. That's an option."

82

She was down in the Valley for the long weekend visiting her mom and doing other things. He asked her to meet him on 246 right after Santa Ynez High School across the street from the church. He was waiting at the entrance to Quail Valley Road. She pulled in and rolled down her window.

"Follow me," he said.

And he crossed over 246 onto Marcelino Road and took a right on Janin and a left on Entrance until it ended on Krill cul-de-sac and they parked and they got out of their vehicles. He out of the blue '98 Ranger and she out of that Subaru.

"You've never been here before?"

"No."

"I used to do daycare at that church sometimes."

"Isn't that a Mormon church?"

"I have no idea. I think I only went a couple times. The only memory I have of it was once when I didn't feel that good and this woman gave me a tums or something just, like, right out of her purse and I told my mom about it later and she was really pissed. Not at me but... Anyway..." As he was saying this, they were stepping closer to each other. Closer. And closer. And their breath was in the air breaking apart and binding and separating and rising up and confronting. And at that moment they stood in front of each other. And in the next moment they embraced and then let go. "I never knew this place existed, though. My parents showed it to me. They watch the fireworks from the high school up on the bluff on the Fourth of July."

He was feeling good. He was feeling confident. Yes. She met him. And he remembered the conversation he'd had with his friend from high school who'd known her longer than he had, and he felt that he maybe knew her better than she knew herself and with that feeling, he led her from their parked cars at the end of Krill cul-de-sac where the fig tree embraces the ground with a twenty foot circumference but bears little fruit. And through the fence to the private land, he led her up the trail to the right where the hill is and the oak trees that are about one hundred years old, that lay their burdened bodies close to the ground. Because the comfort of death calls those trees as clearly as gravity or roots.

And in a few short minutes they were at the top of the bluff where there was a bench facing out to another inlet and another opening with a slope and a bottom and a dry riverbed and grape arbors and across that dry riverbed another slope rising upwards, sprouting dark plumbs of oak crowns among barren, brown grass until the sky voices pale blue and the wisp of clouds are horsetails among an endless backdrop.

And they sat on that bench and he told her his tale:

Our lives are parallel. It doesn't matter what we do. We will inevitably come back together. There is something here for us. Some reason that we are set up this way. We have to play this thing out.

She just listened and looked out over the opening and toward the dry riverbed. There wasn't anything for her to say. And he looked at her face and saw her moving toward the mountains and the sea and something else entirely, but in that moment, he only felt his own words and his commitment to them. He believed them. And he looked out over the slope and toward the dry riverbed with her, but they looked at different things.

After a time they got up and walked back to their cars and he was feeling light and playful and rubbed against her as they walked and kissed her cheek and she was feeling frustrated and said she just didn't understand.

"A couple weeks ago, you said you didn't feel like we could talk for a while and you needed space. I'm just not understanding." And she whined it a little but also said it sort of like a stone would say it or maybe concrete or something solid and cold and unmoving and impossible to get to.

And he noticed. He noticed it all and he just kept a memory of it for later. Because in that moment and the one that followed when they hugged and they both drove out onto 246 and she turned left and he turned right, he was still emboldened by his own story. When he created it and formed it in his mind, it filled him and now that he had said it out loud, in her presence, it had left a glow that stayed slick and white and shining into the evening when the night came and that's when he noticed it slowly begin to fade.

He fell asleep in his little studio in Santa Barbara and dreamed about death again and when he woke up the glow was gone and replaced with sorrow and embarrassment and it was only then that another story began to emerge. It smoothed and rounded and shaped itself as he got up out of bed and moved and walked and sat down on the beach in the cold, damp sand.

I am not yet who I am becoming.

And this was something he had felt many times but never really accepted. But that day, with the waves and the smell of seaweed and salt, he did. He understood that he was not broken - but that he was also not whole. He understood that he needed time for solitude and emptiness and reconstruction. He understood that he needed to learn to be okay with loneliness and more importantly, he needed to learn to be okay with being alone. *Space,* he thought. *From everything except myself.*

He stayed on the beach for a long time. It was not comfortable. And at some point he got in the cold, dark water, naked, and swam out far enough so his feet couldn't touch the ground and he moved his hands and he whispered to himself,

I am in the water.

83

I was alone for a while. Not completely alone. I "dated" - or something like that. I saw people. I made love. I had touch. I shared words. I had conversations, which always included a caveat that I was trying to be alone, in the sense that I was not looking for a partner. In the sense that I was becoming what I was not yet and that I knew I needed space to do that. And I'd say that in so many words. And first that was uncomfortable to say out loud.. But each time, it was received in such a way, I was left feeling that I probably cared a lot more about it than anyone else did. That maybe my assumptions about relationships and the path they were expected to follow were really my own and a bit stuck.

I began to see that relationships were simple. Powerful but simple. Complex, even, but simple. And in that simplicity there are simply a couple of humans with some needs and some desires, negotiating getting them met. There is a forest of trauma and pattern and protection and defense, but there is also a place of sunlight and soft moss where you can just lay down for a while and give and receive love. Simple. This was something you and I had, I think, at least in the beginning and at least for times here and there as the forests of our past grew up around us and began to take over; we would find ourselves there in that sunlight and that soft moss. And lay down together and just be.

During that time I began to form a relationship with myself. As clumsy as I had been when I went on that first date after we separated, I was ten times more so when I reached out to myself and said something like, *Hey, let's hang out. Let's get to know one another. What do you like to do for fun? What are you excited about? What are you needing?* But over time, the path toward self-connection became more sure-footed and I traversed it in sprite and spirited ways.

I did strange things like Gestalt work, where I set up an empty chair and talked to someone who wasn't there. I wrote letters to my child self. I cried and held myself crying and I taught myself how to be both mother and child. And so much more. Countless acts of service to myself. Countless attempts of access. Countless hours of sadness and confusion and clarity and awe and opening. And this was a lonely time for me. Perhaps the loneliest time for me, because I did not run from it. I invited Lonely in and made tea and slept next to him at night and woke up and looked into his eyes in the morning.

I started going to therapy, too, at a clinic right there in Santa Barbara. It was an extension of a school where the students could get real-time work in their last years and it was cheap and it was nearby. At first I had an overweight black guy who wore glasses and seemed not to care a whole lot about the work. I didn't blame him. I was there to talk and I did. I talked and I even cried once. But after a few sessions I got switched to someone else without explanation. Perhaps I was too much for this guy, or maybe the new guy just needed some clients. Either way, I got switched.

This new guy was a Mexican gangster who grew up on some tough streets in Los Angeles and wore Dockers and a button-up shirt tucked in with a belt but his tattoos still snaked out onto his knuckles and his neck. I knew he was a gangster because he told me he was. One day I arrived and he had a black eye and broken lip and some scabs on his fists and he told me he'd had to do what he had to do. He was down in his old neighborhood and his cousin was getting some shit from some homeboys and that was that. He spoke in accented English and when he really got into an idea, his language became rough and he would lean forward and throw his hands around like he was rapping. I loved him. And I felt that he really cared about me. Once I cried and he gave me a pillow to hug and to speak to. He told me there are many ways to live life. He didn't believe anything was wrong with me. That isn't to say, he didn't believe I was in pain and needed healing. He just didn't see me as broken. And over time I could see that much of what he was sharing with me, he was also sharing with himself. He was, in his own way, becoming something he was not yet and I think that is why I loved him and how he helped me. He was who he was in the process of something beautiful. He was, for me, a reflection.

I started writing again. I wrote poetry. Endless poetry. And I kept a journal. And I made lists. And one day I thought about relationships and I thought, *I need to get clear on this*. And I took a long time. Days maybe. And I wrote a list. It was a short list of requirements for partnership. I know you would like to know what they are and I'd love to share them with you. But, honestly, I don't remember any but the first one:

1) *Wants children*

I knew it was not enough that they simply want children, but that they want them in the way I had learned I wanted them - with all the love possible and without force and without laying our traumas and burdens upon them and if we do, to recognize it and apologize. I had been reading a lot of books on parenting and the developmental minds of children and it helped me see some ways I was led to the place I was led and it also gave me a way to actively participate in fatherhood while I slept with Loneliness every night.

Although I can't remember the full list, I know it was potent. And it did something to me that solidified intention and awareness and removed compromise and settling and when, later, I found a French-Chinese girl that was beautiful and sweet and met some criteria on the list, but not all, it allowed me to see the ways that I would later compromise myself for her. And I left.

The same day I broke up with her, I had a therapy session. I planned it that way. And I went in and I told him I needed to end it and I was all anxiety and fear and he just listened and told me there are many ways to have a relationship and I laughed to myself and remembered when our therapist said the same thing years before in Northampton. I can't say it was particularly helpful at the time, but it was one of those moments when no one can help you but yourself. I told her and she locked herself in my bathroom and didn't come out for hours.

A few days later she flew back to France and I got on a plane with Loneliness and we went to a hotel in Bangkok and we lay down in bed together but he was different. He was still Lonely but he was also resolute and didn't need to curl up on me while I slept. He just turned his back to me and got a pillow for his knees and went to sleep. I feared I would be alone forever, but I also knew I would not be. .

(talks with you)

"How is it to be back in LA?"

"It's good. It's so nice I can stay with our friend's parents right now."

"Yeah. It's nice you're so close."

"I know. And it's easy. I know it here. Plus, it's cold in Mass."

"How's the place in Turners?"

"A mess. How's Belchertown?"

"Yeah. A mess."

"You want to come down next weekend?"

"Yeah. I'll come down Saturday."

"Okay. See you then."

85.

(talks with you)

"You want to hold her?"

"Of course. Wow. Look at that little face."

"Yeah."

"She's beautiful."

"Yeah. I told her you're her uncle."

"Yeah, that works. We can make it more complicated when she's older."

"Exactly."

"How are you?"

"Tired."

"Yeah, I bet… Damn. What a precious little thing."

86.

(poem)

i am a slender one at times hiding in the trees
and i am good like the earth when i want
thick strong and loud holding the axe on my shoulder
with a jolly laugh at the work day toil and
i am quiet and small in the ferns wanting women
or a cloud to carry me away or a storm that never
ends
and drowns the world

He drove to LA. She was staying at a friend's parent's house up in the Hollywood Hills. It took about two hours to get there. He drove up a windy road off 405 where houses started small and grew bigger as he ascended and around each curve he caught glimpses of the valley until he rose high enough where it just opened up for him. And he was reminded of that winding road somewhere in Los Angeles back when they were sixteen and had just met a couple weeks before in that poetry class at California Summer School for the Arts. When he had forged his parents' signatures so he could leave the month-long boarding school during weekends and he would take off with new friends that had money and cars with no tops and she would come with him. And they would drive around LA and do cocaine in bathrooms in fancy restaurants and walk around the strip and drink at house parties for celebrities and get kicked out of house parties for celebrities and that one night when the moon was out and big and bright and around a curve when the sky opened up and the valley opened up and he took her hand. And they just held hands that night for an hour or so until they reached their next destination and took some E or read poetry to each other and met someone's famous artist parents or slept on the floor of a house in Topanga.

He arrived and parked on a curve and walked down a narrow driveway and she let him in. No one else was there for the night but in her arms, something moved. They hugged and he felt the gentle warmth of a newborn. They went inside where the house opened up, right was the kitchen and left were the bedrooms and straight ahead was all glass and a door that led to a hot tub and small backyard and deck. It all looked out over the vastness of people and houses and trees and snakes and birds and movement and work and disruption and solitude that is a city. They sat down in the living room next to those windows where the ceiling forgot the attic and just peeked into the sky through a foot of insulation and wood and asphalt shingles. The room was warm and the light was a yellow brown and the couch was a dark and quiet red.

She asked if he wanted to hold her. He did. And she brought her to his arms and he took her up and cradled her. Her little head lay, eyes closed, in the crook of his bicep and chest and her little legs wrapped in a whispering blue blanket in the crook of his other arm. And he positioned her in a way that her weight lay against his chest and heart and stomach. She was asleep and beautiful and white like the moon and the warmth from her was like drinking tea and he felt it in his belly and his blood.

"What a precious little thing."

And she wiggled and yawned and breathed out and he could smell her breath.

This book is dedicated to those I have written about.
Thank you for helping me become who I am.

Made in the USA
Coppell, TX
10 January 2020

14319383R00129